ALBA HOME FOR CHRISTMAS

A ROMANTIC COMEDY NOVELLA

WANDERLOVE ITALIA
BOOK 1

LEAU MACY

*For Karla, the Queen of Christmas, who spreads joy and
encouragement in all seasons*

"Oude liefde roest niet"
Old love does not rust.

-Dutch expression

PART 1

UTRECHT, NETHERLANDS

CHAPTER ONE

FRIDAY, 13 DECEMBER 2002

The bell above the door in our favorite sandwich shop rings, momentarily distracting Ingrid and me. A pair of students from the local university step in from the cold, shaking the wet off their coats and hats. We should have gotten a table farther from the door.

Winter here in Utrecht brings cold rain and short days to the holiday season. In the spirit of *gezelligheid,* we make up for it with cozy comforts indoors and millions of lights along the canals and cobblestone streets outside, but what I wouldn't do for some of the snow or sunshine they get in other places.

"And then what did Henk say?" Ingrid asks. She takes a bite of her *broodje,* the very picture of self-assuredness.

"He said that he thinks we need to break up. That I'm too young for him."

"What are you—thirty?"

"Thirty-one."

"So not exactly a newborn," Ingrid says.

"No. Obviously. But maybe he has a point? About him being too old?"

"*Voorzichtig met je woorden!* Remember, Henk and I are roughly the same vintage. I know you are not calling *me* old," she says, teasing.

"Stop it. You know you will never age. I am fairly certain you're a vampire."

She smiles as if she has a secret. Normally, I'd laugh—Ingrid is genuinely funny—but my laughter is a well gone dry at the moment.

"Why is the age difference coming up? It never seemed to bother either of you before. Has something changed? Or did something else happen?"

"I asked him to go with me on this next trip to Italy."

"Oh," Ingrid says. "For the 'Christmas in the Langhe' article?"

"Yes."

"Okay. Now I am beginning to understand." She shoves her plate away from her and dabs at the corners of her mouth with her napkin. She leans back in her chair and eyes me. "You should know by now that the only two places Henk ever wants to go are to that damn Castle de Haar and home. It drove *me* crazy after a while, but, of course, that wasn't the only thing that did."

I take this all in. Because Ingrid isn't just anyone. She's not just my friend. And she's not just my boss at *Wander-Liefde*, the popular travel magazine where we both work. She was also Henk's fiancée once upon a time. She introduced us, in fact. So if anyone has an insight into my situation, it's her.

"Is there something else you're not telling me?" I ask. "If so, please just say it."

"We both know that while Henk is far from perfect, he's still wonderful."

I raise an eyebrow.

"Don't give me that look," she says. "Just because I can acknowledge that he's wonderful doesn't mean that I think we were right for each other. Henk and I might be closer in age, but you two are *so* much better together. He and I should've just stayed friends instead of even fooling around with the couple nonsense. It wasn't for us."

"Well, Henk doesn't seem to think the 'couple nonsense' is for us, either." I push away my own plate, my sandwich mostly untouched, which is saying something. Usually I have the appetite of a harbor seal.

Ingrid holds her chin in her hand and shakes her head no. "No. This is foolishness. Anyone can see how crazy he is for you. He never looked at me like he does at you. *Ever.* Not even at the beginning. And I know *I* never felt as smitten for him as you seem to be."

I shrug and say nothing, not entirely trusting my voice. I'm afraid anything I say will bring the tears I've been holding off.

"My breakup with Henk might have been incredibly amicable," she says in a musing tone, "but it doesn't mean I didn't leave him with a few scars. Maybe this is all that's going on? Who knows? I do know that he is one of the most stubborn people you will ever meet."

"So what should I do?" I ask Ingrid.

"What can you do? You can't force someone to be with you. You can't get older overnight, and he can't get younger. All you can do for now is take him at his word and go on this trip. Focus on your assignment and take a break from each other. Maybe it's the best thing for both of you—to have some space and do some thinking. About what you really want. About what's really true. Maybe you will both be a little wiser afterwards."

She stands up and shrugs into her coat. "Come on,"

she says, pulling on her hat. "Let's get back to the office and see where we can sneak in some upgrades on your trip. It's the least I can do."

PART 2

TORINO, ITALY

CHAPTER TWO

MONDAY, 16 DECEMBER 2002

After an overnight ride from Amsterdam, my train approaches the Torino station. I stretch and look out the window. The sun is fixed comfortably in the sky here. Even though there's a gauzy grayness obscuring it right now, it still feels brighter and lighter than back home in the Netherlands, if only by degrees. This is Northern Italy, not Positano or Capri. The snowy alps curl around this part of the country, and the feeling here is more of a snowy winter wonderland than a sunny escape. More Austria than Greece. It's impossibly beautiful.

I packed more heavily than I usually would. I really haven't taken that many longer train trips, but I always allow myself a little extra than I would if I were flying. It's so much easier to manage on a train. Especially since the magazine is springing for a private sleeping unit.

Now, however, I look a little enviously at my fellow travelers moving around more easily with only a single piece of rolling luggage and a small backpack. Between my laptop (convenient, but *so* heavy), camera equipment (including tripod—no photographer assigned to this story), and my different outfits for each place and activity, I'm out of breath toting my mountain of luggage down the steps and onto the platform.

I make my way through the modern station toward a section resembling a mall, with restaurants and stores ringing a large atrium. Somewhere a busker with a guitar plays a sweet, spare version of "Oh Holy Night" and the notes echo off the hard surfaces, wrapping everyone in the soft sentiments of the season. I can't see who or where this person is, but I can tell I'm getting closer to the source.

The crowd shifts, and I glimpse the guitarist and catch my breath. His resemblance to pictures I've seen of Henk in his twenties shocks me. His gorgeous face isn't so much a mask of concentration as a look of absolute fascination and... affection? He's watching his fingers dance over the strings with an obvious adoration for the sound they're making. It's an expression of wonder that I think of as being reserved for gazing upon first loves and newborn babies. The audience feels incidental to the experience the guitarist is having. I almost feel like I've intruded on a sweet, intimate moment.

His fixation on the notes allows me to stare at him without being noticed. The similarities between him and young Henk really are unnerving. He looks to be about my age, though maybe a few years younger. His lips are slightly parted. His strong jawline curves up, and I find myself wishing I could cup it in my hand while I taste those lips.

He glances up, and I feel caught. I flush and startle, dropping one of my bags off my shoulder. I bend down to scoop up the few things that tumbled out, glancing up to see his eyes lock on mine.

Oh, shit.

I've heard of love at first sight, which I feel certain this is *not*. But lust at first sight? *Maybe.* A first for me.

I stand up quickly and start walking in the direction where I hope the car rentals are—

And immediately run into a tiny, elderly Italian man, who I send flying backwards onto his bum. I'm not overly tall for a Dutch woman, but I tower over this poor man. He's on the ground flustered and shouting at me—or perhaps just the whole situation in general—in a hoarse staccato of words that I can only assume are being artfully punctuated with curse words. If so, he would be completely justified in doing so.

I put my bags down to offer him a hand up, which he takes reluctantly. I do my best to apologize in the little bit of Italian I crammed while on the train, but it comes down to just repeating "*Scusi*" and "*Mi dispiace*" one too many times for his liking. He hobbles off with his bags and what scraps of dignity he had left after being laid out by an apologetic girl with a double Dutch braid.

I hazard a glance toward the hot busker, who seems to be oblivious to the scene that just unfolded. His focus is back on his fingers and the wondrous music they produce. No more looks in my direction, smoldering or otherwise. At least I avoided *that* bit of trouble. Maybe in more ways than one.

CHAPTER THREE

I taly may be the home of the Slow Food Movement, but that mindset absolutely does *not* extend to their driving. In the Netherlands, we're accustomed to cyclists everywhere and we have a fondness for following rules, traffic and otherwise. Navigating my tiny rental car through the streets feels like a video game I'm ill-prepared to play. The other cars jockey in and out of the lanes and into the smallest parking spots with the confidence and ease of professional drivers.

By the time I arrive back at the hotel after a dinner out, I need a long soak to settle my nerves. From here on out, I'll minimize my city driving wherever possible. I would say I miss my bike, but biking here would also be nerve-racking for me, though the Italians seem to do just fine on their bikes, Vespas, and motorcycles.

I wrap myself in the hotel robe and my hair in a lush towel. I drop into the chair by the telephone to call my mother, making good on my promise to let her know when I arrived safely. Mam regales me with stories from shopping in the Christmas market with Grootmoeder yesterday. We're laughing at a story about Grootmoeder traumatizing some well-meaning vendor when Mam suddenly remembers how expensive international calls are. She thanks me for letting her know I'd made it to Torino and wishes me a fun, safe, productive trip. The line is dead before I can even say thank you.

I didn't sleep that well on the train last night, and it's catching up with me, but I hate going to bed with wet hair. I blow dry my hair and let the day's events unspool around me. The hot busker at the train station, who looked eerily like a younger version of the very man I'm trying *not* to think about, felt almost like the universe is playing a prank on me. I push both him and Henk out of my mind and instead draft different versions of the opening of my article in my mind to distract myself.

Clean, dry hair handled, I pull out my cellphone to charge it and text Ingrid letting her know that I'd made it with a simple "Here."

A message dings back a moment later.

Mam refuses to get a cell phone or to use it for texting. (Henk, too, for that matter. It was a point of contention between us.) Ingrid is a texting savant, however. I can picture her fingers flying over the buttons on her phone. I've gotten better at mashing the number buttons over and over again to select the letter I'm looking for, but I often overshoot and have to go all the way around again. I'm no match for Ingrid's speed.

How was the trip there?

Train good but driving is intense

You'll get used to it

If I live that long ;)

LOL

How's the room?

I will describe it in my article as sumptuous

That's a good word

Only the best for our readers

I weigh whether or not I should just stop things there, but go ahead and text again.

Should I call Henk?

Absolutely not. Take the break. Do your job.

It's so strange not to say goodnight to him

You'll get used to it

Is that your advice for everything?

It's usually right

LOL

You're in ITALY. Enjoy it!

Gotta run. Enjoy the fancy hotel. Let yourself think and have some fun.

There's a lot to unpack there, but there's no point responding with anything other than a quick thanks. I put the phone down and inhale and exhale slowly once, take in my surroundings.

The Hotel Victoria Torino is gorgeous, of course. My room has lots of red wallpaper, heavy curtains and linens, and a fireplace. A highly rated boutique hotel where the influence of the French is obvious. Unsurprising, given that

France is just on the other side of the Alps, and that this part of Italy used to be part of the Savoy Empire.

It's a sumptuous blend of Italian and French influences, designed for comfort. It only highlights the internal discomfort I'm feeling at the moment. Everything around me screams "leisure and ease," but I feel anything but relaxed.

The desire to call Henk, to tell him about my day, is strong. I want to wish him goodnight as I curl up in his strong arms and hear him whisper the same thing he does every night before we go to sleep: *"'Trusten, lief meisje."*

I snap off the light and bury myself under the soft blankets, searching for the path to sleep and the reprieve I desperately need from those words echoing in my mind.

Good night, sweet girl.

CHAPTER FOUR

I browse the Torino Christmas Market, firing off shot after shot with the digital camera Ingrid sent me with to get pictures to go along with my feature article. There are dozens of square, simple whitewashed open stands with peaked roofs. They're decked out with greenery and twinkle lights and big paper snowflakes that dangle from the rafters. Each specializes in some form of holiday gifts, food, or drink. Long red rugs lie atop the cobblestone of the piazza, creating paths between the stalls that funnel shoppers past the various delights.

Under the blue sky, I weave through the crowd and browse wooden cutting boards, bowls, and chessboards; leather purses, belts, and hats; intricately shaped bottles of wine and olive oil; sparkling jewelry and ornaments; and an array of chocolates, cheeses, pastries, and pretzels that boggle the mind.

I love my job.

I pull out my small notebook and take notes on the things that won't show in the pictures. The smells of the baked goods mingling with the green wreaths and wax candles and lavender sachets. The sounds of the canned music and of children running around and laughing, playing tag and angling for sweets. The impossible softness of the cashmere sweaters and hats. I'll do my best to describe these things, the way they complement one another and compete for your attention.

Tucking my camera and notebook away, I pull out my wallet and buy a variety of chocolates. I'll sample some later and write about them for the daily blog. Then I'll take the rest home. I can't resist the urge to buy extras of the chocolate with pistachios, even though I know it's foolish. Henk loves pistachios almost as much as I love chocolate, and old habits die hard.

I walk, snacking on a bar of chocolate, when I hear the clean notes of an acoustic guitar. I follow it, half-wondering if it could possibly be the same busker as last night. Already thinking what a pretty picture he would make for the article if it *is* him, I dig out my camera again and accidentally smear chocolate all over the sleeve of my coat.

I try to find an open space to put my things down and get reorganized, but there are people everywhere and not a spare inch on any of the counters at the booths. I stop near a wall and try to shuffle things around while leaning awkwardly and balancing stuff between my knees and teeth and feet—anything to free up my hands so I can return everything into the appropriate bag or pocket. Finally, I have a system that makes it possible for me to access the camera without massive chaos each time.

Whew!

I shake my hair back, rub my forehead for a moment, and take a deep breath to recenter myself before reentering the fray of the Christmas shoppers. I follow the sound of the guitar music like one of those old cartoons where the character floats along through the air following a scent.

I come around the corner, and there he is again. Soft brown eyes, wide shoulders curved forward toward his guitar, big beautiful hands dancing over the strings, and those gorgeous lips curled inward in concentration.

So far I haven't heard him sing once. Not in the train station and not here. He lets the guitar command center stage, offers only jazzy variations on Christmas favorites interspersed with songs that sound vaguely familiar, but with a twist. I snap a few shots of him. Seeing him through the lens brings him that much closer. He looks up and it feels like he's looking straight at me. Again, I feel myself blush, which just makes me feel ridiculous. Obviously, he's not looking at me.

But when I lower the camera, there he is. And for the first time, I see him smile.

As the Americans say, "Houston, we have a problem."

But is it a problem, really? I'm single now. And this is nothing but a harmless appreciation for a handsome man. *Het log will look wat.* The eye wants something, too.

———

I LINGER until he takes a moment to fiddle with the frets on his guitar. I approach him, telling myself it's because I need his permission to include his likeness in the article, though I will afford few other people in my photos this courtesy. I convince myself that I'm only getting his name and a few small details for the caption to the picture. Or perhaps as part of another side bar or blog post on the Christmas performers.

"Caio," I say, approaching him, starting from the default position that he's Italian, though I feel more and

more certain that he's likely American or perhaps British. *"Come stai?"*

"Bene, grazie," he says, and indeed his Italian is heavily accented. *"Parle inglese?"*

"Oh, yes, I do," I say. "Far better than Italian, actually."

He looks relieved. "Fantastic."

"I thought you might be American," I say, recognizing the accent.

"What gave it away?"

"I don't know. A certain... confidence, I suppose."

This makes him bark out a small, rueful laugh.

"I said something funny?"

"Kind of, yeah."

"You don't think you're confident?"

This makes him laugh again, but lighter this time. "German?" he asks me.

"No!"

"Dutch," he says quickly and points at me like he's just worked something out.

"Yes. What gave it away?" I say, mimicking him.

"Directness, which is another form of confidence, I think. But with some humor mixed in and just a hint of sarcasm. At least that's been my experience with the Dutch so far."

"Yes, that's the official Dutch recipe. I'm Melina," I say, holding out my hand to shake his.

His big hand wraps around my gloved one, and I can feel the warmth of it through the thick knit.

"Andre. *Mi piacere.* Ope. Sorry. That's Italian. Habit. *Aangenaam,* Melina. Did I get it right?"

"Yes. Flawless Dutch. Nice to mectcha," I say. "Did I get that right?"

"Oh, yes. Very American sounding. Nice job," he laughs. And this time, it's looser, musical in its own right.

"I don't mean to interrupt your session. I'm here working on an article for a travel magazine. I took a few photos of you playing just now. I wonder if you'd mind being included in the photos accompanying the articles. And if so, could I get some more information from you?"

"Sure and yes, though, would it be possible for you to hang out for just a few more minutes? I only have a few more songs, and then I'll quit for the day. Can I answer your questions then? I want to take advantage of the crowd before it thins out."

"Of course. I'll come back by when you're finished."

He looks down at his guitar for a moment, fiddles with the frets again, plucks a few strings, then looks up at me through thick lashes, "Why not stay and enjoy the music?"

I flush again. This is getting out of control. I push down the coltish feelings threatening to turn me into a fawning girl—surely not the first one to fall prey to Andre's charms. Henk springs to mind, unbidden. They may look alike, but the flirting that comes so effortlessly to Andre is something Henk would never do. I square my shoulders and start backing away. "I'll keep an ear out. I won't go far."

As I put some space between us, Andre plays a rousing version of a song with a sultry undertone. It takes me a second to recognize the American Standard, "Blue Christmas."

CHAPTER FIVE

"So how did you become such an expert on the Dutch, Americano?"

"Andre," he says and smiles that damn smile again. It really is powerful.

"Okay, so how did you become such an expert on the Dutch, *Andre*?"

He talks while he finishes packing up his stuff. "I've been traveling since the summer. Mostly throughout Europe. You start to get a feel for people and where they're from. It's a little like being back in the States in that way. Like when you can tell that someone's from The South or New York or California. There's just a vibe."

"Where are you from in the States?"

"Bloomington, Indiana. Born and bred."

"Indiana. I'm not exactly sure where that is. Somewhere in the middle of the country, though, right?"

"There's that directness again. Yep, sort of in the middle. Kind of halfway in between Chicago and Nashville."

"I didn't realize those two places were close to one another."

"They're not, especially by European standards. They're a good day's drive apart from each other, but they're both 'only' about four hours away from BTown."

"BTown? I thought that was Boston."

"That's BeanTown. BTown is just what the locals call Bloomington. You know a lot about America."

"My father lives there." He looks tired, I realize. And a little distracted. I should wrap this up. "So are you traveling alone, or are you traveling with friends? And have you been busking long?"

"I'm traveling alone. Been busking here and there for most of the time but really kicked it into high gear around the holidays. It's been fun to play at the Christmas markets."

"You're good. And you make it a happier place."

"It's already a happy place, I think, but glad I can add a little something."

"Will you be here through the holidays or heading back to America?"

"I'm not sure yet."

I feel like I'm prying, so I offer him a quick exit from this line of questioning. "A man of adventure."

"That's me," he says. "Listen, I would love to chat, more than you realize, but if I don't get going I'm going to be stuck in one of the bad bunks at the hostel for tonight. I'm happy for you to put my picture into your article. That's actually very cool. What do you need from me?"

"Oh, if I could just get the spelling of your name and the place you're from, that would probably be enough. If you want to include your email address, the magazine could reach out with anything else they need." I hand him my notebook. He puts his guitar down, takes my pen in his left hand, and starts scratching out his details on the page.

"Can you read my handwriting?" he asks.

Andre Thompson
Bloomington, Indiana
athomps27@indiana.edu

"Yep. Thanks, Andre from BTown," I say and hold up the notebook.

"All good? Need anything else?" Andre asks, and I could swear he's looking for me to come up with something.

I shake my head slightly and blink, bringing myself back to the moment.

"Oh. No. I'm all set. I put my email in there in case, like you said, you…or the magazine have any follow-up questions," he says.

"I saw that. Thank you."

"Well. I'm going this direction. How about you?"

"No. I'm the other direction. Hotel Victoria Torino."

Inside my mind, I slap my metaphorical forehead. *What was I thinking? Why would I tell some stranger where I'm staying? Pull it together, Melina!*

"I knew I should've been a journalist. You must have fancy article money," he says. His tone suggests he's trying to put me at ease for my *faux pas* without ignoring it completely.

"Now who's 'direct with a hint of humor and sarcasm?'"

"I didn't say the Dutch had the corner on the market," he says.

"Well, goodbye. Best of luck, and thank you for agreeing to the photos."

"My pleasure," he says. "Best of luck to you, too." He turns to leave, but stops. "Just one thing," he says, pointing toward a spot on his own forehead. "You have a little something here on your forehead. You can hardly tell out here, but I thought you'd want to know before you got back to the hotel."

"Oh," I say and rub at my forehead. "Did I get it?"

"No, I think it might be dried on there. Did you have some chocolate earlier, maybe?"

I close my eyes, and nod, remembering the chaos of earlier, of trying to get myself rearranged, the shuffling and the chocolate bar I'd sampled. I've likely been walking around with this smudge of chocolate on my forehead for some time.

"Here," he says, stepping forward and tugging gently on my hat so it comes down just a bit lower. "Presto! Solved."

He's just in front of me, and I realize that I can smell him, the confluence of all the different products he uses, the scent of his wool coat, and just... him. I haven't been this close to a man other than Henk in a while. Now that I can see him up this close, I'm guessing Andre's younger than I thought. Probably not long out of university.

"*Bedankt*," I say. "Thank you."

"You're welcome," he says and looks at me a beat longer than is strictly platonic, before hustling off toward his hostel. I stand frozen to my spot and watch. He spins around once before disappearing around the corner. "*Buonaserra*, Lois Lane!"

CHAPTER SIX

WEDNESDAY, 18 DECEMBER 2002

I arrive in Piazza San Carlo, AKA Torino's "living room." It's famous for hosting an array of concerts, markets, and other events year round, but for now, the immense square is peaceful. The lightest of snow is spitting, and people are ambling about. In the distance, a three story wooden advent calendar has eighteen windows already opened. A fire truck with its ladder extended sits in front of it. I watch as a firefighter opens up the nineteenth window. I can't wait to come back tonight when the windows of the calendar are actually lit up. And I hear the laser light show is spectacular.

The four-story buildings ringing the Piazza offer protection against the wind, letting the weak winter sun that peeks out do its best to warm the space, despite the temperatures and the light snow. I wander toward the enormous bronze statue in the middle of the piazza, which I know from my guidebook the locals call *"Cabal ëd Brons,"* which is a local dialect called Piedmontese for "The Bronze Horse." I like that the Torinesi offer a tip of the hat to a language spoken mostly by elders and those in rural

areas these days rather than refer to it in the more domi-
nant Italian.

I snap a few pictures of the statue, though it remains
unadorned, and therefore Ingrid almost certainly won't
choose it for the article or the blog post. I can't resist. From
everything I've read, this statue has been the center of
innumerable victory parades and celebrations and one of
the most popular rendezvous points in the city. *Ci vediamo al
Canal ëd Brons! See you at the Bronze Horse!*

And right now, I'm feeling more than a little lonely,
which rarely happens to me this early on these sorts of
trips. I chalk it up to sleep deprivation. For the second
night in a row, I'd resisted the urge to call Henk. I was
rewarded by dreams of the confusing, chaotic variety. In
them, Henk and I are having dinner under a flickering
light, and he keeps changing ages every time the light
shines back on him. Henk as a boy, as an old man, as a
young man, as a baby, as the forty-eight-year-old man I'd
met and fallen for. As a corpse. And I try to make sense of
what he's saying each time, but it's confusing, almost a
different language.

Rather than marinate in my misery, I choose forward
motion.

I'm too late to see the celebrations that happened
around the Feast of the Immaculate Conception. The
L'Immacolata Concezione, a national holiday here, always
takes place on December 8th. Many families choose to put
up their Christmas trees and *presepi* (nativity scenes) that
day. The construction of the *presepi* is such an important
tradition here that it's even spawned a cottage industry.
Some communities seek the guidance of a *presepista* to help
them create their nativity scenes.

I meander around the city in search of more examples
of the *presepi* and other decorations. The range of these

displays astounds—everything from tradition and realistic to cartoonish and avant-garde.

I check my watch to confirm what my stomach is already telling me. I allow myself to make my way to Caffè Platti. I've been told it has the best *Bicerin* in town. A layered drink made up with a base of espresso, a thick layer of hot chocolate, and topped with lightly whipped cream (or milk, for those who want it a tad less rich), *Bicerin* is a local specialty that demands coverage in the article. It's exactly the sort of thing Dutch travelers are bound to love and likely to be one of my favorite parts of researching the article.

Caffè Platti sits at an intersection mere blocks from the train station where I arrived. It's the corner business in a long string of them, which are all connected by a covered walkway of arched stone. I read that some royal or another from the House of Savoy ordered the porticos and mall-like arcades built when they ruled over this area so that they wouldn't get wet when it rained.

People bustle in and out through the huge, old-fashioned door to Caffè Platti. I wade into the stream going in and find myself in a room that looks like a small shop. Two counters mirror each other, one on my right and one on my left. People line up at the one on my right, ordering and downing Italian espressos in one gulp before dropping two coins on the table, and offering quick, friendly *ciao's and grazie's* on their way out. The space has the feel of a tiny busy train station.

The counter on the left isn't actually a counter at all, but a row of glass display cases offering tantalizing finger foods. Traditional Piedmontese pastries that suggest both French and Italian influences are closest to the register, followed by an array of chocolates, and the "Torte Platti" signature cakes they're known for.

At the far end of the case, closest to the tiny hostess stand at the entrance to the dining room, dozens of kinds of tiny, triangular sandwiches are on display. I peruse these *tramezzini* while I wait for someone to come back to the hostess stand.

To my right I hear someone say, "I should've pegged you as someone smart enough to find their way here. How's it going, Lois Lane?"

I turn and see Henk's younger doppelgänger grinning that confident American grin at me.

Here comes trouble.

CHAPTER SEVEN

A harried waiter comes up and says, "This way, please" before depositing us at a two person booth in the corner. Andre gives me the couch side. From this position, I can see the whole dining room, which looks like something out of a storybook or a vintage music box.

Chattering people fill small tables and booths in groups of two and three. Small tiered plates sit in between them loaded with the same treats found in the front display cases. Everywhere, people are savoring their *Bicerin* in small, round, clear mugs or out of little espresso cups and saucers. Ornate mirrors and baroque touches give off a feeling of comfortable opulence.

"So, what's good?" Andre asks.

"You're the one who's been here. I should ask you."

"This is my first time in the dining room. I usually just come in for *un caffè* and get back to it. I don't really let myself ogle the menu too much."

"Why not?" I'm suddenly concerned that he won't be able to afford his bill and expect me to pay.

"No time, usually. And there's also a kebab place around the corner that I've hit a few times. More protein. I'm sure all these little sandwiches are good, but I'm guessing they won't keep me full all day."

"Are you typically out there all day?"

"I mean, there's really no 'typical' to it. I'm pretty much making it up as I go along."

"How did you get started busking?"

"You have a really great vocabulary, by the way."

"Thank you."

"It's impressive. Really. Most people just say, 'playing guitar' or 'panhandling' maybe. 'Busking' isn't that common a word, even for Americans. Anyway. To answer your question, I met a guy at a hostel earlier in my trip. He had a trumpet with him and would go out and do a few hours to get extra beer money for when we went out. I started going with him *et voila!*"

"How long have you been traveling?" I ask.

A different waiter comes over before Andre can answer. He takes our orders and scoots away. Andre takes off his coat and settles his chin into his hand, looking at me, squinting playfully. "You ask a lot of questions."

"Well, I am a journalist, after all."

"What else are you?"

"How do you mean?"

He sits back, brings his hands together on the table in a loose knot. "I mean, are you a reader? A runner? A pet owner? An amateur bassoonist? Former bullfighter? Exiled royalty, perhaps?"

I laugh. And he keeps on.

"What about someone's girlfriend?" He looks down at his hands for a second and then back up at me.

My breath catches as our eyes lock for the third time

since I first saw him. (But who's counting?) I feel the flush start from my stomach work its way all the way up to my scalp. In this light, I have no hope of him not noticing my raging forest fire of a blush, given my fair complexion. It seems to unsettle him, too. He talks faster now.

"And I don't see a ring, so I'm guessing you're not a wife. Or a mother. Although, you know, I suppose you don't have to have a ring for that. Anyway. I'm babbling. I'll stop now."

He leans back and laughs once. Softly, nervously. "Sorry. None of my business."

"No," I say. "It's okay. To ask. We're a direct people, remember? Though I never talk about my bullfighting days. That topic is off limits."

We both laugh louder at my feeble joke than it deserves, relieved for anything to release the tension.

"So?" he says.

"I am no one's wife or mother, and I was someone's girlfriend. Until very recently."

He just nods.

I redirect back to Andre before he can react any further to what I've said. "What about you? What else are you besides a guitar man?"

"You mean besides exiled royalty?"

"Yes, obviously."

"Is this on the record?" he teases.

"I don't know. Are you ever going to answer the question?"

"No."

"'No' you're not going to answer the question or 'no' you—"

"No, I don't have a girlfriend. At least I don't think so. Not anymore. But maybe?"

He presses his lips together and shrugs his shoulders. It's obvious he's trying to be breezy or even stoic about it, but the embarrassment and misery underlying it is also evident.

I struggle with what to say next. Part of me wants to confess my own confusion about my situation with Henk. Part of me wants to offer him some sort of encouragement or soothing words. And part of me is just overcome with a blinding curiosity. That part wins.

"'Maybe'" I say. "What happened?"

"She left me at the airport right before we were set to go on an around the world trip we'd been planning for more than a year."

"*Wat de hel!*" I say.

"Yeah, not great."

"Why?"

"She got into Harvard Law School off the wait list. It was a whole last-minute thing. She had like a day after getting the news to accept or pass. So she accepted the admission and passed on our trip."

"How long ago did that happen?"

"What is it now? December 18th? So three months and twenty-one days. But who's counting?"

"Wow!" I say. "So she's supposed to be here now?"

"Yep."

"I'm so sorry."

"Thanks."

"Wait," I say. "You said, 'Maybe?' What does that mean? Is there a chance that she'll still come? Is that why you're not sure if you're broken up?"

"I don't really know what to think."

"So will you see her over the holidays?"

"I'm not going home for the holidays."

"So, when will you see her then?"

"That's the question. We didn't break up *per se*. We just chose to not go where the other person was going. So it's almost like we're apart more than that we're not together, if that makes any sense. Does that translate?"

That sounds sort of familiar.

"Yes. I think I understand exactly what you mean."

CHAPTER EIGHT

THURSDAY, 19 DECEMBER 2002

Following one last, longing glance at the Hotel Victoria Torino, I climb into my car. The next phase of the trip will take me to another boutique hotel. This time, though, I'll be staying in the picturesque countryside.

As much as I love the vibrancy of a city—I'm a Utrecht girl, after all—I'm very much looking forward to the quiet of the countryside. I've rarely spent more than a day or two away from my native environment, where you can usually count on a bare minimum of bustle.

I'm scheduled for just over a week at the Villa della Nebbia in the Langhe region of the Cuneo Province. I'm curious about what it will be like for me to actually spend time so much time in the quiet.

I imagine slow, luxuriously slow, starts to the day, while I sip my coffee and journal or just stare contemplatively at the gorgeous views.

Just me.

Alone with my thoughts.

For a week.

O nee.

The downside sometimes of being a solo travel journalist on an assignment is that it allows for a *lot* of time alone. The accommodations are nicer now thanks to my job, but they don't lend themselves to the sociability that hostels offered when I was younger.

Although, to be fair, I don't have a lot of experience with hostels. While my friends were busy hopping on trains—often in pairs or small groups, but sometimes even solo—I was spending vacations visiting my dad and his new wife in Alabama. From what I could tell over the years, the only thing my American father likes more than convenience is the radical *inconvenience* of moving house every few years into a newer and bigger house. Sometimes with a new wife in tow, sometimes not.

I *do* have a fair amount of experience visiting hotels on vacations with my mother, though. And the situation at the Torino hotel seemed very much the norm. Almost everyone else there had been traveling with at least one other person. I have to assume it's going to be the same thing again at the next one.

I think about bumping into Andre yesterday. How nice it was to just… chat with someone. Especially someone somewhat close to my age. I realize just how rare it is for me to spend time with people my age or younger. I've always been a bit of an old soul, but especially lately when my days are mostly filled with my coworkers, Ingrid, Mam, Grootmoeder, and… Henk.

An idea strikes me. I remember the hostels I stayed in having bulletin boards where people organized shared rides. I pull out my guidebook and look up the map of Torino, trying to spot the nearest hostel. One called "Combo Torino" looks promising and not too far out of my way. At the very least, maybe I could give someone a ride to the next city and enjoy some conversation on the way there.

A nice, distracting chat will help set you straight, Mel. You're just a little lonely.

The thought that maybe I can help someone seals it for me. I'm doing it. I know Ingrid told me to come here and do some thinking, sort my mind out, but everyone has their limits. My thoughts and I need a chatty chaperone to give us a break from one another.

———

I KEEP the page marked in my guidebook with my left index finger, while I steer with the rest of my fingers on that hand. My right hand is busy with the stick shift. My eyes dart everywhere at once as I maneuver through the traffic toward the hostel. A couple times I have to flip the book open to doublecheck the correct places to turn.

Maybe this is a bad idea.

Fate smiles upon me, and I find a spot to park. I'm grateful I know how to drive, but even more grateful that I rarely have to do it in the city back in the Netherlands. This is so much harder than bicycling. I take a deep breath and hop out of the car before I have a chance to talk myself out of the whole thing.

It turns out the bulletin boards are outside, which is another stroke of luck. I don't even have to go inside, which felt a little intimidating, if I'm being honest with myself. I peruse the boards like I'm window shopping, keeping an eye out for people who need rides. There aren't as many as I expected, but I suppose it is the holidays. And the Langhe region isn't as much of a tourist hotspot as Tuscany or Venice or Rome. The few requests are hoping to ride to places much farther than I am going. Most are requesting Italy's more famous places or transportation to somewhere in nearby Austria or France.

And really, what was I thinking? That I would just show up and someone would be ready to hop in my car on a moment's notice? I'm leaving today. What are the chances that someone is just sitting around waiting for an opportunity to catch a ride to a place that's less than two hours away?

I resign myself to the idea that the drive will be a quiet one. That's what radios are for, after all.

I walk back toward my car, taking in one last view of this new-to-me corner of Torino, a city which has more than met my expectations. The Christmas lights above, now unlit, bring back the magic of the light show from this week. I gape up at them.

I look down just in time to see the panicked expression on a woman's face right before I smash into her stroller.

CHAPTER NINE

It's one of those giant, old-school, baby buggies that you only see in cartoons and old movies. I bounce off of it like a rubber ball.

I manage to catch my balance by grabbing onto a light pole, but I'm still reeling. The Italian mother is gesticulating and speaking at me, in an (understandably) perturbed, rapid-fire, and (very) loud voice. I'm apologizing in some combination of Dutch and English and Italian. It takes me a moment to settle down enough to notice that there isn't actually a child in the buggy, but instead a slew of packages and Christmas decorations.

The woman backs up the stroller slightly and maneuvers it around me. When I know that she is safely past, I break into laughter and quickly move my hand from my chest to my mouth to try to trap the sound.

A voice from behind me says, "You just make a point of running into people or what?"

I jump half out of my skin and turn around to see Andre smiling one of those big, gorgeous American grins at me.

"What in the world are you doing here?" I ask.

"This is my hostel. What are *you* doing here?"

"I'm just—hey, wait. What do you mean do I 'make a point of running into people?' Who else have I run into?"

"Do you mean besides that poor guy you put on his ass at the train station?"

"You saw that?" I open my eyes wide, and my mouth drops open in shock. I smack him in the place where his shoulder and his chest come together. It's like hitting a tree wrapped in a wool coat. "I can't believe you saw that and didn't say anything before."

He cops a comical scowl and rubs the spot where I hit him. "Ow."

With no better response coming to mind, I laugh and shove him again. I can't tell if this is adrenaline I'm feeling right now or the resurgence of my silly crush. But then is there any actual difference between the two?

"Well, I mean, you can understand why I didn't say anything before," he says. "I don't wanna get laid out. You're a force of nature."

I cover my eyes, shaking my head, and then peek through my fingers. His comical scowl is gone, and the grin is back.

"So, were you putting something up on the boards or what?" he asks.

"No, it's stupid. I'm getting ready to go on to my next part of the assignment, and I thought maybe someone would want a ride to one of the places out in the direction I'm going. But everyone wants a ride to Paris or Capri or something."

"I'm sorry to see you go," he says, and I think he means it, but probably only in the way that an American would. It's not that he's being insincere or fake, but Americans are quicker to friendship than people from most countries. Certainly faster than the Dutch.

"Don't worry. There are plenty more like me around here," I say.

"I'm not sure you're right about that." He says it and chews on his lips just enough to be…flirting with me, maybe?

I'm not quite speechless, but all I can manage is, "Well, I should go."

I start down the sidewalk, walking fast, as if I can outpace the feelings that are creeping up on me whenever Andre's around. I'm not sure what to think of them, but they feel risky. And I don't do risky.

"Hey, Lois Lane," Andre calls out. "There's no chance you're heading to Acqui Terme, is there?"

I stop short for a second. I recognize the name from my itinerary, though I think I'm not scheduled to do anything there for another day or two. I spin around to face him, but keep walking backwards toward my car and away from him. "No. My next hotel is out in the country."

This has the benefit of being technically true, but I still feel a twinge of guilt at my evasiveness. *Maybe I'm not as direct as I think of myself as being?*

"It might be out that way, though," I say, cleaning my conscience. "But I'm leaving right now. You probably aren't ready to go right this very minute, anyway."

"I mean, I could be. It would take me, like, five minutes to pack up my stuff and check out. *If* you're going that way, that is. No pressure. I just thought maybe…"

"Maybe what?"

"I don't know. I thought maybe it could work out for both of us?"

His sentence is technically a statement, but it comes out as a question. One I don't know how to answer. Our time together at Caffè Piatti has been one of the highlights of the trip. Really, almost every one of my favorite moments so far has involved this stranger and his ever-present guitar.

He talks faster, maybe sensing my weakening resistance to this idea. "You'd be saving me a loooong bus ride. There isn't a direct train there, so if I don't catch a ride with someone, I'll have to take a train all the way down to Genoa and then take a bus back up from the coast. Totally crazy route."

I sigh. "Where did you say it was again?"

"Acqui Terme."

I walk the rest of the way to my car and pull out my guidebook, flip it open to the map, and scan. I must make a face because he reacts instantly.

"Too far out of your way?" he asks. "That's okay."

"No. *Het is lood om oud ijzer.*"

"Okay, but I don't know what any of that means."

"It means 'it's lead to old iron' or—"

"Still not helping," he says, teasing.

"Be quiet long enough for me to tell you!" I say and laugh.

He grins again, but this time, it lights up his entire face. Like a little kid. The deal is as good as done.

How can I deny him a lift now? How could I make that hopeful look disappear?

How can you walk away from the opportunity to spend more time with him?

The truth of that last thought hits below the belt.

"It means that it makes no difference. I can go that way or the other way. It's the same distance for me, really."

"So…are you up for some company while you drive?" he asks.

"I was planning on listening to music while I drove there."

"I could work with that," he says and lifts his guitar case slightly. "I can't sing for my supper, but I can strum for my... chauffeur."

I raise my eyebrow at him. "Chauffeur?"

"I couldn't think of anything else that worked with 'strum.' And, c'mon, it almost rhymes with supper. You gotta give me points for that."

"You have ten minutes, and then I'm leaving with or without you."

He takes off on a dead run into the hostel, and I can't help but laugh again. It feels good. I haven't laughed since... the last time I was with Andre.

CHAPTER TEN

Andre comes sprinting out with a huge backpack and his guitar. A look of relief washes over his face when he sees me still sitting in the car parked out front. He slows down, but only barely.

I hold up my wrist and point to my watch, pasting on a deadpan expression I hope comes across as funny. He teased me mercilessly the other day about the Dutch and our penchant for promptness.

He throws his head back and laughs. Slowing down another gear, he's still speed walking to the car. He opens the boot of the car and drops in his backpack. The whole car rocks.

"What have you got in that bag?" I ask. "A dead body? You're not exactly traveling light."

"You're one to talk," he says, loading his guitar into the backseat before sliding into the front passenger seat. "There wasn't much room in that trunk. You brought a lot of stuff yourself, I see."

"At least mine didn't make the car drop ten centimeters."

"What can I say? I don't have a lot of baggage, but what I have is *heavy*."

From our conversation the other day, I feel like this has a double meaning, probably referring to his girlfriend abandoning him at the airport, but I don't ask him about it. Directness is one thing. Cruelty is another.

"You can be the navigator," I say, handing him the map.

"I can do that. Before we go too far, though, let me ask. How do you want to work out my share of the trip? Do you want me to buy a tank of gas or do you have a set amount in mind? What's best for you?"

"Normally, we'd just split it—"

"Oh, right. Go Dutch. Duh. I should've known."

"Oh, right. American throwing his money around. Should've known," I say sarcastically mimicking him.

"Okay, fair point. Truce?"

"We'll see how long *that* lasts," I say and roll my eyes for comic effect. "To be honest, don't worry about it. The magazine is paying for everything on this trip, so it would be less complicated for me if I just pay for the gas. I don't want to figure out how to account for your half when I get back and am sorting out expenses."

"You could just pocket it."

"That's not how I do things. Don't worry about it. It's my treat."

"Can I at least buy you lunch or something?"

"We'll see. I'm not sure we'll need to stop. It's not that far if we drive straight there."

"Is that how you always travel?"

"What do you mean?"

"The most direct way there? No diversions?"

Once again, I'm not sure we're talking about the trip. I

keep my eyes on the road, almost afraid to look at him and see my suspicions confirmed about a second meaning.

"Well, that's the best way to avoid getting lost."

"But what if getting lost is the best part?"

PART 3

THE LANGHE COUNTRYSIDE

CHAPTER ELEVEN

I drive the route that takes us through Asti. The fog is burning away as we approach it on the A21 Motorway, and the snowcapped Alps stand like regal giants in the distance.

"That never gets old," Andre says, pointing with his chin.

It's hard to believe that I'm here in this place. Even in the cold hibernation of winter, the rolling hills are beautiful. Imagining the verdant green of vineyards isn't difficult.

I really should insist that Henk come back here with me at some point when it's warmer.

The thought comes to my mind before I remember that at the moment Henk has no intentions of going with me anywhere—not now, and maybe not ever. Or being with me in Utrecht, for that matter. I focus on my attention on my stomach, hoping to drown out my thoughts.

"I was thinking about stopping in Asti for lunch. What do you think?"

"I think that sounds great," Andre says. "I've been curious about it the whole time I've been here, honestly.

We used to have these commercials on TV when I was a little kid. Did they have those in the Netherlands, too?"

"Do you mean 'Reunite on Ice?'" I ask, recalling the old advertisements of couples gallivanting all over Italy and holding up glasses of wine and just smiling, smiling, smiling.

"'Reunite on Ice…so nice!'" he says in a cheesy announcer voice. "What was the other one? It was like that."

"'Do you mean Martini & Rossi Asti Spumante?'"

"Yes!" he says and his eyes widen as it comes back to him. "It would be this couple, and the woman would say, 'I love this champagne' and then the dude would say, 'No, it's Martini & Rossi *Asti Spumante*.' And she'd insist it was champagne. And every time his voice would get tighter and tighter, like he was getting seriously pissed. You never saw them. It was always just the bottle and the glasses of wine or whatever."

Andre laughs at the memory. "'*Martini & Rossi **Asti Spumante**.*' Man, that would crack me up every time. That guy sounded like he was about to *lose it* and start busting up some cases of sparkling wine."

"That sounds menacing. Weird strategy for a wine marketing campaign," I say.

"Good point. Still, if they have it on the menu, we'll have to get it."

"You can get it, but I'll be driving."

"One glass won't hurt."

"Probably not, but I'd rather play it safe."

"Do you always?"

"Do I always what? Drink Martini & Rossi Asti Spumante? No."

"Okay, smartass. You know what I mean. Do you always play it safe?"

"I'm here in the car with a strange man I didn't know a week ago, so I'm not exactly afraid of my shadow, but yes. Usually, I do play it safe. In the Netherlands, we believe that rules are usually there for a reason."

"Let's hear some of these rules," Andre says.

"You tell me some of your rules."

"I asked first."

"Fine. I'll play along. Well, to start with, I'd say the first rule is 'Be Direct and Honest.'"

"Yes. Directness has been well-established."

"And honesty."

"Yes, *honesty*," he says. And then somewhat under his breath, "Or bluntness. Tomato, to-mah-toe."

"What does *that* mean?"

"You know 'busking' but not 'tomato, to-mah-toe?'"

"Just tell me!"

"It's a little like your 'old iron for lead' or whatever you said earlier. Like 'same difference,' with a little 'agree to disagree' thrown in. In this case, I'm saying that sometimes your honesty veers into *brutal* honesty."

"But it's still honesty," I say, and raise my finger into the air.

"Yes, that is undeniable. What else?"

"Okay, rule number two: always be on time."

"That's another one I already knew. Why do you think I was hauling ass out to the car? I knew you'd leave me if I was a minute late."

"Maybe," I shrug.

"Probably."

"Okay, probably," I admit.

"What's number three?"

I search my brain for the sorts of things we take for granted as being true back home in The Netherlands.

"Have you ever heard about that thing the Japanese say about how the nail that sticks up gets hammered down?"

"No. Sounds brutal, but I think that I get the gist."

"We have something a little like that, but less intense. We just say, '*Doe normal, dan doe je al gek genoeg.*' It means, 'Act normal. That's already crazy enough.' You don't have to make a spectacle of yourself. Or flaunt your wealth or brag or pretend to be something you're not. Just be yourself."

"I like that."

"Really? I sort of think that's the opposite of what someone like you would like."

"Why's that? Is it because I'm a musician or because I'm Black or because I'm American?"

"I don't know. Probably a little of all of them. *Definitely* because you're a musician and an American. Americans love standing out. That's why people sometimes think you brag too much and you're a little fake."

"Wow. Tell me what you really think."

"I didn't say *I* think that about all Americans or you, in particular. I'm just answering your question. But, come on. Every time I see you, you're playing in front of a bunch of people. You don't mind standing out."

"Oh, okay. So you don't have artists and musicians in the Netherlands then?"

"Of course we do. And we have mixed feelings about them. We respect the hard work and talent that it takes to become good at something, but then we don't like people who show off about it too much or think they deserve special treatment."

"How in the world does *that* work?" he asks.

"Okay, one example. Van Gogh was Dutch. He started painting because he was a minister's son and they couldn't spend money on wallpaper. So he painted a design for them. Or maybe they just didn't want to spend the money.

I can't remember which way the story goes. But either way, they didn't spend it. And then he worked very hard and got very good, which we would admire. But then he cut off his ear," I say, and shrug.

"Oh man, talk about showing off," Andre says.

"Exactly. Total show-off move."

"Okay, I think I get it. What about the Black thing? Where are you on that?" He looks at me warily.

"Well, to me, one of the reasons why everyone likes Black culture so much and tries to emulate it, is because it's more demonstrative, in general."

"Another good word."

"Thank you."

"So all Black people are demonstrative?"

"Well, okay, obviously not. Individuals are different, no matter what group you're talking about. I'm talking about as a culture, in general, but even then, it's degrees of openness, depending on where people live. My ex-boyfriend is Black, but he's also Dutch. And that makes him a little more reserved than some of the Black people I've met in Alabama, where my father lives, for instance. People are very friendly there. And you—you're somewhere in between."

"That's because Hoosiers are 'Midwest Nice' and people from Alabama got that 'Southern Hospitality.'" He says the last two words in a twangy voice that sounds nothing at all like the soft lilt I've heard from actual Alabamans when visiting.

"But under it all," I say, "no matter where it is, there can often be a warmth or a sparkle or a *je ne sais quoi* among people in Black communities that's very, very appealing to people. It stands out. People are drawn to them like moths to a flame. So that's what I mean, I guess."

I think about Henk's family, who've been in The

Netherlands for generations on both sides. They're Dutch, through and through, but they're Black, too, and the blending of the two cultures is just one of the things that makes them so special. The idea of not getting to be around them anymore makes me sad all over again. So much light going out of my life.

"*'Je ne sais quoi'*? Did you just swear at me in French?" Andre teases, and I snap back to the conversation.

"No, but I can."

"I'm sure you can, but how does that fit with your rules?"

"Totally within the rules."

"Seems weird."

"Not to me," I say and smile widely.

"Your ex is Black?" Andre says after a bit of quiet. "Didn't expect that."

"Being normal and not standing out is important, but Dutch people also don't like hierarchies. We try to treat everyone the same, no matter how different we are from each other. We don't always succeed. There are still problems, of course, but we do our best. We have lots of different types of people in Utrecht. Henk happens to be Black. I happen to be white. That's all."

"That sounds nice."

"So you're liking my rules now?" I say.

"I mean, I like *that* one. I think you guys could ease up on the obsession with punctuality a little, but keep going. I want to hear more."

"I don't know how many more I have."

"Well, what's keeping you from having wine with me at lunch?"

"Okay, that one is about being self-sufficient and practical. If I drink too much at lunch, then I won't be able to drive us on to where we're going."

"But one glass—"

"Okay, yes, one glass probably wouldn't hurt, but I'd rather just not worry about it one way or another."

"Fair enough."

"And besides, that leads us to my last rule."

"I'm on the edge of my seat."

"We're pretty frugal."

"Oh, disappointing."

"Why do you say that?"

"Because I already knew that one. Everyone knows that one." The conversation dies off. I follow the signs toward's the center of Asti, figuring we'll find somewhere good to eat there.

"Henk, huh?" Andre says out of nowhere. "That's your ex?"

"Yes," I say and resist with all my might the urge to shift in my seat. "You look a lot like him, actually. Well, a younger version of him."

"Really?" And then after a pause, he says, "Huh. I did not see that one coming."

"Which part?"

"All of it. Just… all of it. You're full of surprises, Lois Lane."

CHAPTER TWELVE

A ndre convinces me to drink a glass of wine after all,
convincing me that I needed to experience an Asti
Spumante in the place it's named after. We order one as
an aperitif and clink our glasses together. The flavor is
sweeter and fruitier than I usually drink, but it's not cloy-
ing. I don't mind it. I wonder if this could be another side
bar or blog post: "Whatever happened to Asti
Spumante?"

Andre and I split a platter of Piedmontese starters: thin
slices of *vitello tonnato*, a tender veal draped in a creamy,
tangy tuna sauce, along with a small serving of *carne cruda*,
raw beef seasoned with olive oil, lemon, and a pinch of
salt, and finally, roasted peppers topped with a drizzle of
anchovy-garlic sauce.

I order *tajarin al burro e tartufo*, a handmade pasta tossed
in butter and topped with white truffle shavings. Andre
choses *brasato al Barolo*, a slow-braised beef dish cooked in
Barolo wine, served alongside a serving of creamy polenta
that soaks up the rich, velvety sauce. The waitress suggests
bonèt, a traditional Piedmontese pudding made of choco-

late, amaretti, and rum. And who am I to walk away from a suggestion as good as this?

I insist on a walk after lunch to revive myself. After all that rich, delicious food, I could use a nap, but I still have a ways to drive before that can happen.

We leave the trattoria, which is tucked into a narrow cobblestone street. The soft winter light filters down between the strings of lights strung between the buildings. Andre and I take turns pointing out the few ways that Asti, a smaller, medieval city, and Torino, a bustling city with an eclectic array of architectural styles, are similar and the variety of ways they are different.

We wander back to the car. It's less than an hour to Acqui Terme from here, but I don't want to push my luck. It's probably almost another hour after that to my hotel in the countryside near Sinio. I can feel myself itching to get back on the road.

"This has been great, but it's time to go," I say.

Andre looks a little sad, and I realize I am, too. Once we get in the car and I drop him off at his hostel, odds are that we won't see each other again.

Unless we make plans to see each other.

We're both going to be in the area, after all.

I *could* see if he wants to do any of the experiences with me. The *per diem* budget the magazine gave me is stretching a lot farther than I need for just one person. I may have forgotten an item or two when I packed to come here, but my frugal ways travel with me always.

All during the drive to Acqui Terme, I consider asking Andre to join me for the cooking class I'm signed up for. Then it dawns on me. I have no idea why he chose to come to Acqui Terme. So I ask.

"There's a luthier out here that I read about. I'm hoping to meet him," he says.

"What or who is a luthier?"

"It's a guitar maker. Well, actually, any stringed instrument. But this guy specializes in guitars, which obviously interests me."

"Hey!" I say. "You were supposed to provide the music on this drive. 'Strum for your chauffeur,' I believe you said."

"Busted. The truth is, it's really hard to do that in these tiny cars."

"Okay, fine," I say with a wave of my arm.

"You'll forgive me for my breach of Rule #1: Be Direct and Honest?"

"Yes, this time."

"But not next time?"

"What?"

"You said 'this time.' Does that mean there'll be a next time? Because I can say, I wouldn't mind spending more time with you if I had the chance," he says.

I flush again, but I keep my eyes on the road. Instead of responding to that, I seek the safety of a question. "So why do you want to meet this luthier?"

I won't spare a glance his way for fear of what I'll see on his face, but the disappointment in his voice comes through, anyway. "Oh, I just love being around other musicians and craftsman and people who just love the instrument. Sometimes guys like that will also have some work they'll let you do under the table."

"Do you know where to find him?"

"I mean, not really. Acqui Terme is all I knew for sure."

I shake my head.

"Hey, we can't all be planners. Some of us fly by the seat of our pants a little more."

"I'll say this: you've clearly found something you feel passionately about."

"My guitar is the only woman that has never let me down."

The reference to his girlfriend is right there. I'm about to ask, but then decide to take a different tack.

"The *only* woman who never let you down? So no sisters then? And what did your mother and grandmothers do to be such disappointments to you?"

"Okay, maybe not the only woman. Family doesn't count."

"Pretty sure it does."

"Well, I just meant women I've been involved with romantically."

I scrunch up my nose. "So are you saying that you and your guitar are romantically involved?"

"Okay, hold up. No, that's not what I said—"

"Are you having sex with your guitar, Andre?" I tease. Sometimes a little profane humor distracts and resets better than anything.

"Ha, ha. Very funny. You know what I meant."

"Does she have a name?" I ask.

"Of course."

"Are you going to tell me what it is?"

"I'm debating it."

"Do you want to tell me her name or do you and she just want to walk the rest of the way?"

"Hello, Aggressive. Fine. It's Stella."

"I like it. Like the character in *A Street Car Named Desire*?"

"No. As in *How Stella Got Her Groove Back*. Angela Bassett, man. I have a hardcore crush on her."

"What time is your reservation with the hostel? When do you have to be checked in by?"

"Oh, I don't have a reservation."

"What?" I say, aghast. "So you don't have a reservation at the place you're staying tonight. And you don't have a way to find the man you came here to meet?"

"I'm sure it will be fine."

"But what if it's not?"

"Then there are other hostels. Or hotels. I'll figure something out. I always do. And I'll find him. It'll all work out."

I shake my head, marveling at his *laissez-faire* attitude about it all. I would be anxious without a confirmed reservation. "I just assumed you called or emailed before you left the last hostel."

"When would I have called? You mean in the few minutes I had to pack up all my stuff, checkout, and get out to the car?"

I think about offering my cellphone to him, but think about the roaming charges and figure that we're close enough now it won't make any real difference, anyway. "I hope you're right."

CHAPTER THIRTEEN

He wasn't right.

The first hostel was full. As was the second one, which was also the only other one in town. Small hotels are scattered around, but with the holidays, they've all been full or incredibly expensive. I could've left him to figure this all out on his own, but when I imagined him hiking around town with all his stuff when I could so easily drive him, it felt wrong.

Also, I can tell that Andre's nervous about the price of the remaining hotels. My guess is he didn't plan for this possibility, and that it's blowing a sizable hole in his budget.

More to the point, if I'm being honest with myself, it's mostly that I'm dreading dropping him off.

I look at my watch and calculate when I'll get to my hotel at this point. I don't want to push it much later. I don't know what the roads between here and there are like, but I'm not keen to find out in the dark. I want to get going. "Listen," I say. "I have a crazy idea."

"I'm pretty open to any ideas right now, crazy or other-wise," he says. "I'm starting to think my best bet is for you to drop me off at the train station, and I'll get a ticket to somewhere bigger with more options."

"How about you just come and stay with me?"

I've heard of double-takes, seen them in movies, but I've never seen one in real life. They're far funnier in person than I ever would've guessed.

"Don't get any ideas. I'm not asking you to go to bed with me. It's just that my suite at the hotel where I'm staying next has a sitting room with a couch. You're welcome to it."

Andre wears the yearning he feels to take this option all over his face. Clown makeup is more subtle than this expression, but still he says, "Are you sure about that?"

Am I sure? No? Yes? Maybe?

"Yes. This is getting ridiculous. As beautiful as Acqui Terme is, I'm tired of driving around it. Ideally, I'd like to get to the hotel before it gets dark."

"All right, then. Let's go," he says, and the relief in his voice is audible. "Just for tonight. I'll get myself sorted out by tomorrow, I promise."

"I'm not concerned. It will all be fine."

"Can I pay you for my half of the room, at least?"

"No, because—"

"The magazine."

"Right," I say. "Andre, don't worry about it. Really. It's not a big deal. I have to come back out this way tomorrow for a cooking class, anyway. I can drop you back off here or even take you to somewhere else nearby. Maybe you'll have more luck in Alexandria."

"If you're sure, then let's do it. Thank you so much."

"You still have to navigate, though."

"You really are intrepid, Lois Lane," he says, opening up the map and squinting at it in the dying light.

"I have a question. Why do you keep calling me that?" I ask.

"What? Lois Lane?"

"Yes. Why do you keep calling me 'lazy clay'? That's not really an expression we use. Does it mean something in the U.S."

"Lazy clay? What are you talking about?"

"Are you not saying *lui leem*?"

"I'm saying, LO-iss LAYne. I don't know what you said just now."

I start laughing, figuring it out, at last. "I thought you were saying, *lui leem*. It means lazy clay in Dutch."

"Why would I be using Dutch?" he says, laughing with me now.

"Why wouldn't you? I'm Dutch. You used Dutch when I first met you. And you seemed like you'd spent time with some Dutch people. I thought you must have picked up some when you were around them."

"No. I barely know the basics. What did you think I meant by—what was it?—lazy clay?"

"I don't know! I just thought maybe someone had played a trick on you at some point and told you it was something we said. Like, 'Oh, when we say goodbye, we say—'"

"Lazy clay?" he asks and then laughs harder.

I snort, and this gets us both going again. Finally, I gather myself. "So, then what *are* you saying? What is LO-iss LAYne? What does that mean?"

He pulls himself back together enough to speak and says, "It's not a what. It's a who. Lois Lane is Superman's girlfriend. You know, the bold lady reporter who works with Superman's alter ego, Clark Kent."

I gave him a blank look.

"At *The Daily Planet*?" he says.

"Oh, now I know what you're talking about."

"Really?"

"NO!" I say.

After another fit of giggles out of both of us, I say, "Oh, I'm not really into superheroes."

"Wait, wait, wait. I mean, there's 'not into superheroes', and then there's Superman. I thought it was one of those universal things that everyone knew about."

"Oh, you Americans."

He smiles and looks out the window. After a few moments, he says, "Well, for a girl who isn't into superheroes, you're doing a good job of playing one right now."

CHAPTER FOURTEEN

The roads to the hotel are, in fact, full of hairpin turns and steep inclines. I can't decide if I'm glad that we got going while it was still light or whether driving up in the dark would've made the journey less scary.

When I saw that the hotel I would be staying in was an *agriturismo*, a villa nestled amidst a farm, I pictured a place in a valley. But this one perches atop one of the "hills" that would be considered a mountain where I'm from.

Italian farms—more often than not vineyards or hazelnut groves in *this* part of the world—make use of every available scrap of land. The precipitous drop from the side of the road is enough to make me grip the steering wheel with a death grip. When I look down, however, I see endless rows of grapevines clinging to the side and houses perched here and there amidst them.

"You good?" Andre asks. I glance over at him for a moment, noting his wide eyes. "Nothing to see over here. Keep those eyes on the road."

"It's beautiful. Even in the stark winter. I can't imagine how breathtaking it must be in the other seasons."

"Yes, gorgeous. I'd just rather it not be the last thing I see before I die. At least not anytime soon. Feel free to slow down."

"I'm already going below the speed limit. Rule followers, remember."

"Really? It feels like you're going kind of fast," he says. "These roads are something else."

"You don't have roads like this back in Illinois?"

"Indiana. And no. I mean, I live in Southern Indiana, so there are some curvy roads, but nothing like this. You?"

"In the Netherlands?" I scoff. "No. Absolutely not. It's flat. That's one of the reasons everyone bikes everywhere."

"Well, you haven't traveled here before? Or someplace like this? Everything is so close together here. I just assumed."

"My mother likes the sea. We always go to the beach. And my other vacations were always to America to visit my father."

"And you said he lives in Alabama?"

"Yes."

"*Another* thing I would not have called."

"Why's that?" I ask.

"I don't know. I think of Alabama as being one of those places people don't move from or to. How did your parents meet?"

"Long story," I say. "Maybe another time. For now, look up there on the left. Can you read what that says? That could be where we're going."

He checks the printed directions in his hand and looks back up, squinting. "Yep. I think we are here."

"Great news."

"*Seriously,*" he says and lets out a big breath.

"Are you criticizing my driving?"

"Absolutely not. You're my favorite chauffeur ever."

"That's what I thought." I pull into a parking spot and catch a breath, before it's immediately stolen from me when I take in the view. "Wow."

Even as the dark quickly descends, I can see that the view from my stay over the next few days is almost unsettlingly, achingly beautiful. Right now, everything is layered in shades of gray and black, but lights twinkle throughout.

Torino is so wonderful that I hated to leave it. And the drive up here is a tad harrowing, but right now, I am so grateful Ingrid insisted that part of the time spent on this trip be in the Italian countryside.

The hotel isn't actually a villa, but more like an old castle. It only adds to the magical feel of the place. We grab our bags from the car and walk through the huge wooden door and into the cozy lobby, decorated with twinkle lights and greenery. A wood fire burns on the fireside in an enormous fireplace and a couple sits in two chairs near it, sipping something that sends curls of steam into the air.

"Benvunto! Welcome," the man behind the front desk says and smiles. It almost feels just a little too wide to be sincere, but I give him the benefit of the doubt.

"*Buonasera,*" I say. "*Come stai?*"

"I am very well, thank you. How are you this evening?" His English is good, if heavily accented. I can only assume the same can be said about my Italian, which must be why everyone on the trip so far seems to switch to English whenever I try to speak Italian. In Torino, I got so used to everyone speaking English, I often forgot to speak Italian at all, much to my chagrin.

"You are Melina Jansen?" he asks.

"Yes."

"The magazine has taken care of everything. The reservation is for one, but I see that you have a guest. That is no problem. The rate is the same. You will only need to pay the small local tax for the extra guest, but it is only a few euros."

"Perfect," I say.

"We only need to have your passports so we can make a copy of them. It is the law now." Andre and I dig out our passports and pass them over.

"Thank you," he says and disappears with them for a moment through a door behind the desk. I hear a copier running and then he is back. "Here you are, Ms. Jansen. Mr. Thompson. I hope you enjoy your stay. I am Emanuele. Please let me know if there is anything we can do to make your stay more comfortable. Dinner is in the dining hall just through there. We will begin serving in just a few minutes and close at *nove di sera*. Nine pm. Here are your keys. Your room is just up the center stairs and to the left."

"Thank you," I say. *"Grazie mille."* Andre has already shouldered my bag and holds suitcases in each hand. He looks like a pack mule.

"I can help your husband with the bags," Emanuele offers. He looks at my ringless hand when he says it, which feels too coincidental to be accidental.

"I think we have it, but thank you," Andre says before I can set the record straight about who Andre is. I decide to just let it go. Less to explain, and what would I even say?

"As long as you don't mind carrying my guitar case and your backpack, honey?" Andre asks, his eyes full of amusement.

"Yes, completely fine, *sweetheart*," I say, matching his look. To Emanuele, I say, *"Stiamo bene.* Thank you. *Grazie. Buonasera."*

"Buonasera."

———

ANDRE and I dump all our stuff in the two halves of the suite, take turns freshening up in our (shared) en suite bathroom, and head down to dinner, where we proceed to stuff ourselves silly.

Still full and a bit dopey from the spectacular pasta and wine, I collapse onto my bed. This bedroom is even more spectacular than the one in Torino. The fresco painted on the ceiling makes me feel like some sort of royalty from another age. Like something out of a dream.

Andre's sitting room couch is smaller than I'd hoped, but he seems unfazed. He's already pulled the extra duvet out of the armoire and has made up a little bed. The doors separating the two rooms are full of glass panes. Privacy will be tricky here. The huge, old-fashioned key sticking out of the keyhole on the bedroom side seems to work, however.

"Thanks again for this, Melina," he says. I don't know what I would've done tonight, but I know it wouldn't have been this nice."

I grimace and motion to the small sofa. "Are you going to be okay on that? You're going to have to curl up like a woodland creature to fit on that."

"I'll be fine. I've slept in far worse places, I promise."

"Well," I say. "I should go call home. Let them know I made it here safely."

"Do you want me to leave for a few minutes so you can have some privacy while you talk?"

"No. Completely unnecessary."

"Great," he says. "Honestly, I don't think I'm going to be awake much longer to hear much of anything, anyway."

"Okay, then. *Buona notte*, Andre."

"Goodnight, Lazy Clay."

———

"HOW WAS THE DRIVING THIS TIME?" Ingrid asks.

"Good, though these curvy roads are scary at times."

"Please don't drive off a mountain."

"I'll do my best." I fiddle with the cord on the hotel phone. "Listen, there's something I need to tell you about. It's a little bit of a weird thing."

"What is it? Is everything okay?"

"Yes, I'm fine. I wanted to let you know that I met someone—an American—when I was in Torino, who needed a ride to a hostel in one of the cities on the way to my hotel. Long story short, the hostels were all full there, so Andre is staying here in my sitting room for tonight."

"Well, that was kind of you," she says. "Is she trustworthy? You aren't going to wake up to find yourself robbed blind, are you?"

"No, I'm not worried about that. *He* seems very trustworthy and kind."

"He. *Oh*." Ingrid says.

"It's not like that."

"What is it like?"

"We're… friends," I say, realizing that it's actually true. Somewhere in the course of the conversations we've had over the last few days, we went from strangers to acquaintances to friends.

"What kind of friends?"

"The usual kind."

"What's he look like? Is he handsome?"

I pause, trying to think how to answer

"That's a yes, then," says Ingrid. "You said he's American?"

"Yes."

"A handsome American. Uh-oh. Shades of your parents' story, no? What does he do? Is he a student?"

"He just graduated. He's a musician, actually. A very good one. A guitarist."

"You are sharing your *agriturismo* with a handsome American musician? You might as well be in the Bermuda Triangle, my friend. You are about to be lost at sea."

"You were the one that told me to go and have a think. And the reality is that I'm single again, remember? Henk broke up with *me*. If I did want to have a fling, would it be so terrible?"

"Of course, not. Is that what you want?"

"I don't know."

"Where is he now?" Ingrid asks.

"He's already asleep. Right now, I'm more worried about the volume of snoring already coming from the sitting room than about anything romantic happening tonight."

"Oh, *that's* why you're talking so quietly. It all makes sense now. I guess I should let you go. It's getting late, anyway."

"Ingrid, what should I do?"

"What have you been doing so far?"

"Following my instincts, I guess."

"So keep doing that."

"That's your best advice?"

"That's the only thing any of us have got to work with when it comes down to it. Life is a series of events that don't always fit prescribed rules, no matter how much we try."

"Thanks, Ingrid."

"*Veel success, vriend.*"

We hang up, and Ingrid's good luck wishes have me

lying awake pondering my situation. Is meeting Andre a stroke of good fortune or a disaster waiting to happen? Our situation might be unconventional and unexpected, and he certainly isn't in a position to be someone I can rely on, but do I need that right now? And can I really rely on *anyone* besides myself? I thought I could rely on Henk, the steadiest man I've ever met, and look at what happened. Maybe the best thing I can do is just what Ingrid advised, and continue to follow my instincts. I'll take things as they come.

With that, I fall into a deep sleep for the first time in a long while.

CHAPTER FIFTEEN

FRIDAY, 20 DECEMBER 2002

I think I believed until now that everyone was grouchy in the morning. I thought it was a universal law that no one should speak to one another until they have had at least one coffee and a half an hour or more to wake all the way up. Night owls, like my mother, or early birds, like Henk and I—it makes no difference. The rule remains the same. A proper day starts with a wary silence.

Andre believes himself to be exempt from this unwritten law. From the moment he wakes up, he is a bubbling fountain of cheerful chatter. I scowl at him, shocked that he seems to expect a response.

"Do you want to go down to breakfast with me? I was just getting ready to head down. I can wait, if you like."

"No, you go ahead," I say, already looking forward to the rightful restoration of morning silence.

"You sure? Will you be coming down? Or would you like me to bring you back something?"

"I'll be down soon," I say.

"Cool. See you soon," he says and breezes out and has the audacity to have an actual spring in his step.

———

"YOU'RE BACK," Andre says.

"What are you talking about? I've been sitting here with you for the past hour."

"Your body has been plopped into that chair for the last hour, but I don't think you actually occupied your body until a minute or two ago." He slides the moka pot toward me. "Need another hit of espresso?"

I give him a side eye and a half smile. "No, I'm fine."

He'd ignored my earlier statement completely and had brought me back a tray from the breakfast downstairs. A moka pot and an espresso mug. A pair of pastries, along with a cornetto. Little toasts and an array of adorably small pots of jams and honey. Some sliced salami and cheeses and some fruit. He'd even managed to bring up a napkin, a glass of freshly squeezed orange juice, and a set of utensils. He'd already folded his blankets and returned them to the armoire, allowing me the space to perch on the couch and cut a swath through the food he'd brought.

"So what was that, nine cups of espresso?" he asks. He's sprawled comfortably in a nearby chair, sipping his own glass of orange juice.

"No, it was a very reasonable two cups."

He makes a grimace face and holds up three fingers.

"Okay, three. Just as any normal person would require. What are you naturally caffeinated or something?" I ask.

"Pretty much."

"I've heard of people like you, but I always thought they were myths like a yeti or a *witte wief*."

"I know what a yeti is. What's a vitta veef?"

"It's a legend. They can be good, or they can lead you to your doom. It means white woman."

"Did you just call me a white woman?"

"I guess I did," I say, laughing.

"I have to say, that's a first for me."

"I bet."

"No plans to lead you to your doom, by the way," he says. "What do you have planned? When do you want to get rid of me?" His voice sounds overbright, forced.

"I can't blame you for wanting to get someplace more comfortable than the couch," I say and brush the crumbs off my fingers onto the tray. "I can take you wherever you want to go. I don't really have anywhere I have to be until my cooking class this afternoon. Other than that, I was just going to drive around and visit the different Christmas markets, et cetera."

"It's not that," he says. "I actually slept great on the couch. I just figured…"

"What?" I ask, hoping he'll say what I'm thinking.

"That you'd want to get me out of your hair," he says. He rolls his lips inside, which makes his dimples pop. It's his warm, vulnerable eyes that catch my breath, though. I meet them, let myself be transfixed by them for a few seconds.

Oh, well.

"My hair is fine," I say, breaking the spell. "Nicely braided, as you can see."

"I do see. There's nothing penetrating that tight configuration. My mom would be impressed, actually."

I pat my braids, preening. Before I have time to second-guess myself, I blurt, "Andre, I have another crazy idea."

"Hit me."

"What if you stayed on with me for the rest of the trip?"

"For real?"

"Yeah. Why not?"

"What happens if your boss finds out about my being your travel buddy?" Andre asks.

"I told her last night. She's fine with it."

"Really? When did you talk to him?"

"Her. Ingrid."

"Sorry," he says, abashed.

"It's okay. I talked to her last night, though I could barely hear her over the sound of a thousand chainsaws coming from the sitting room," I tease.

"Are you saying I snore? I don't snore."

"*Je snurkte als een os.*"

"Does that mean 'you snore like a horse'?"

"Close. Like an ox."

"I'm calling BS on that. But back to your boss. It's really cool with her?"

"Sure? Why not? It's not as if I'm on some top secret mission for the government. I'm writing an article on traveling to this area during the holidays, and most people reading my article will likely go on vacation with someone. It actually makes it easier for me to see what it would be like for two people traveling together."

"Two people traveling together—a couple?" Andre says, raising his eyebrows.

"Could be a couple. Or two friends. Or you can think of yourself as my work colleague for the next couple of days. Whatever. It'll make it less awkward for me at the hotel, too. If you disappear after the first night, they're going to think I had a one-night stand, or that we had a raging fight and you left me."

"Since when do you care what people think?"

"I told you. I'm Dutch. We don't like standing out. I don't need the extra attention."

"Oh yes, Melina and Her Many Dutch Rules. I nearly forgot."

"So, what do you think?"

"Are you kidding? Totally in. If you're sure," he says. I can see he's holding back that wide, hopeful smile with everything he's got.

"As sure as I'm going to get. I mean, if you don't mind staying on the couch, that is."

"Absolutely. No problem. The couch is great."

"Okay."

"Okay?"

"Yeah," I say, and we both grin. "Though I may doubt my decision by tonight. Remind me to stop for earplugs on our way to the cooking class."

"You got it. They'll be my treat."

"I thought you didn't snore."

"Okay, you got me there."

"See? This is why I stick with my rules. Honest and direct is just easiest."

But the truth is, I'm not being completely honest with Andre. I don't tell him how I keep replaying a snippet of my previous comment in my mind.

On our way.

I like how that sounds way more than I'm willing to admit to myself, let alone to him.

CHAPTER SIXTEEN

We're driving the same route we came in last night, but today the fog that the Langhe is known for is obscuring the view. I drive even slower, but nothing slows the Italian drivers down. I'm passed on curves and on hills. If I lived here, the stress of driving here every day would shave years off my life. Or perhaps I'd just get used to it.

"You know," I say. "I would hate for you to get rusty with you taking some time off busking."

"Yeah? You have a solution to that?"

"If it would help you, you can play for me later."

"Deal."

"Do you like busking?"

He tilts his head and nods. "I always love playing, and I don't hate busking, but I also don't mind saying it: it will be nice to take a break from performing outside for money and just travel for a little while."

"I remember you saying that you sort of fell into busking. What *were* you planning to do this trip?"

"Mostly watching other people play music. We were

going to go to a bunch of jazz festivals along the way. We'd saved for *years* for this trip."

"Your girlfriend—"

"Amber."

"Amber, does she play something, too?" I ask. I feel like I'm trespassing by asking so many questions about her, but I can't seem to resist.

"No, she sings. Has a great voice, actually. We figured that if we got in a pinch, we could busk, but it wasn't part of the plan. We were just supposed to have a big adventure together."

"So what happened? Did you misjudge how much it would cost?"

"Maybe. There are some things that would've cost a little less if you were sharing it with another person, so that's a little bit of it. But mostly I didn't budget the cost of the bender that I went on at the start of the trip when I realized that she *really* wasn't going to join me."

I don't know what to say to that. His last sentence sounds so forlorn. I just want to throw him any sort of lifeline that will make him less sad. "I bet you have some stories."

He chuckles once. "You don't know the half of it."

"I probably couldn't handle even half of it."

"Have you ever done something like that? Gone off the rails?" he asks me.

"Me? You mean besides this?"

"This is you going off the rails?" he asks, a look of shock on his face.

"What can I say?"

"Wow. Okay. So you were right before. You probably couldn't handle stories from my bender."

"Plus, like I said before, when everyone else was taking those sorts of trips, I was visiting my dad."

"In Alabama."

"In Alabama."

"No wild times there?"

"In Alabama?" I ask.

"Why not? I think of them as a state that would know how to throw down."

"Probably. But I was always just with my dad and my stepmother."

"No step brothers or sisters?"

"Nope. I was an unplanned pregnancy. I'm pretty sure he made sure that never happened again." I make a snipping gesture with my fingers.

"It seems like he wanted to be in *your* life, at least."

"We did the bare minimum until we both had decent excuses for not flying me to Alabama every year. He's not a bad guy, just not really cut out for fatherhood. Getting a vasectomy after he and my mom divorced was probably the most responsible thing he ever did. Though it's a little hard not to take it personally."

"How do you mean?"

"Well, you know, he saw me and thought, 'let's not make any more of those.'"

"Or maybe," Andre says, "he thought, 'how could I ever do better than this?' When you get it right the first time, sometimes you just stop there."

"You look good in those," I say.

"In what?"

"Those rose-colored glasses of yours."

"Nah, man. No glasses here." He waves his hand near his handsome face.

"Rose-colored contacts then. Probably a lifetime supply distributed to every American child at birth."

He scoffs. "We're not really big on distributing things to all babies. Too afraid of Socialism back home."

"So everyone needs to get their hands on their own supply, then?" I tease. Everything is feeling too heavy. Andre and I are just supposed to be having some meaningless fun, not solving our problems—let alone the world's.

Picking up on my tone switch, he says, "That's right. Babies gotta come out scrappy." He waves his fists, like a cartoon character spoiling for a fight.

"Well, they get their hands on them somehow. Every American I meet seems to be skilled at looking on the bright side. Even first thing in the morning," I say pointedly.

Andre laughs, and the sound of it, the ease of it, is like a kind of comfort food.

CHAPTER SEVENTEEN

SATURDAY, 21 DECEMBER 2002

The cooking class contains three other couples.

Okay, let me try that again. The cooking class contains three couples and then me and Andre.

Two of the couples are German and one is a Southern Italian/Brazilian combo who met on vacation here the year before.

I wasn't sure how it would go for him to accompany me to this part of the itinerary, but I assumed that he could be added to the wine tour and tasting portion of the day. Fortunately, Giuseppina, the main instructor, and her uncle, Francesco, are more than willing to accommodate one more in the kitchen. Especially when we offer to pay for Andre's session in cash.

We each don our aprons and wash our hands before awaiting instructions.

"Today, we will make a pasta called *tajarin*, which is special to this area. Sometimes you will also hear this called *tagliolini*, but here in the Langhe, we prefer *tajarin*. When you finish, they will look like this." Giuseppina holds up some long, thin, golden-yellow noodles draped over her fingers.

We are standing in a circle in an ordinary farm-house kitchen. She holds out her arms toward the half of the circle and we lean forward to look at them. "To make these, we will use only flour, egg yolks, and salt."

She turns and puts the noodles down on a plate on the counter. "Is everyone ready to get started? Please join me in the dining room."

We file in, each of us stands behind a chair until Giuseppina invites us to sit down. In front of each of us, a mound of flour rests in the middle of a well-scrubbed patch of table.

"Take your two fingers," she says, holding up her index and middle fingers, "and put a little spot in the middle. This is for the egg yolks." I pull my two eggs out of the small bowl they rest in, as instructed. I crack mine and pour the egg whites back into my small bowl, and wait for further instructions.

Andre has already made a mess of his eggs, with a path of spilled egg white marking the distance between the flour and his small bowl. I think of Henk at home on a lazy Sunday, making us *wentelteefjes*, cracking the eggs with one hand before tossing them into the compost. I can almost smell the cinnamon that permeates the air during those times. I shake my head to scatter the thought and drive back the tears that have blurred my vision.

Why dwell on such things now? I'm in the middle of an abso-lutely delightful experience, surrounded by lovely people. Get a grip, Melina!

"Everyone doing good so far?" Guiseppina asks.

"Doing great," I say and covertly wipe at the edges of my eyes.

"Okay," she says. "Next we get our hands dirty. We are

going to use our fingers to toss a little bit of the flour onto the yolks at a time. And then we are going to use our fingers to mix everything together. A little at a time. Yes. Just like that," she says, looking around the room.

"Andre, good job. You have very strong fingers, I think. You play an instrument?" She asks.

Basking in the attention, Andre answers, "Yes, ma'am. Guitar."

"It is useful to you. If you get sick of the guitar, you could be a great pasta maker."

"Why not both?" Andre asks and smiles up at her.

"You are right! Why choose?"

After more kneading than I would have guessed, Guiseppina is satisfied with the elasticity of everyone's dough. She distributes long, thin rolling pins and everyone rolls their dough into what they think are thin sheets of pasta.

After about ten rounds of Guiseppina saying simply, "Thinner," we all have our sheets ready to go.

"For some, they use the pasta machine. This is the fastest way. Or you can fold the dough over like this and then use a sharp knife to cut strips two to three centimeters wide. This is not so fast and requires a steady hand. But we have something that is more fun than that."

She pulls out something that looks like a stringed instrument, like a lute. "This is called a *chitarra*, which means in Italian just like it sounds: guitar. Each of these strings are between two and three centimeters apart, so you don't have to guess if you are cutting the right size. They first used these in Abruzzo, Italy, but now we sometimes use them here, too. You will all try it, but first I will have Andre show everyone how to do this."

She puts the *chitarra* just in front of Andre and helps him to drape his sheet of thin pasta over the wires of the device. "Now, you roll your roller over the top of the pasta."

Andre does and the sheet mostly disappears in the gaps and is collected in the bottom of the device. A few get hung up and refuse to drop. "Now, Andre, it is time for you to do what guitarists do."

Andre strums his fingers gently over the strings, and the last strands fall. The joy on his face makes my heart skip a beat, and as insane as it is, I'm a little envious of that sheet of pasta. I want to feel his fingers on my skin.

Get a grip, Melina. You're all over the place. Settle down.

———

WE FINISH the class by making a silky sauce made up of only butter, garlic, and some of the pasta water remaining after the tamarin is flash boiled for a minute or two. By the time we lay the pasta into the pan, followed by a generous bit of salt and ground pepper, the smell is intoxicating. Giuseppina invites us to sit down at the table in the other dining room, this one is already set up for a feast, with wine glasses and bottles in place.

Giuseppina brings in plates of pasta and Francesco goes around with a black truffle and a small grater. He goes around to each person and shaves a generous portion of the truffles over our full plates, adding an earthy and verdant flavor. The Barolo wine from a local winery does more than bring it all together. It elevates it to the next level. The flavors of the food and wine harmonize on my tongue while I bask in the company and conversation with our classmates.

But I find my eyes drifting again and again to Andre, sneaking visual sips of him. He's so different from Henk, so much louder and younger. Where Henk's passion for things is quiet, steady, and must be unearthed with persistence and patience, Andre's enthusiasm for everything—for music, for the rolling topics of conversation, for the food, for the wine, for the very existence of this place, this room —is endless, obvious, effortlessly shared.

"What do you think, Melina?" Andre asks, catching me lost in thought.

"Oh, it's the best pasta I've ever had. We are clearly naturals at this."

"Right? I mean, I don't want to get ahead of myself here, but we should obviously open up a restaurant. How can we deny the world this food?"

"Absolutely yes," I say, playing along with the joke. "But what about my writing and your music?"

"You can write the descriptions for the menu and articles about the restaurant, and I'll play my guitar for the customers."

"Then who will be making the pasta?"

"Good point," he says. "Sorry, world. We can't do it all. We'll just have to keep all this for ourselves."

CHAPTER EIGHTEEN

The drive home this time *was* in the dark. The one glass of wine I allowed myself at dinner has relaxed me enough that I might actually be a better driver. It's mostly worn off by the time I reach the truly twisty part of the drive, but enough remains to take the edge off my usual death grip on the steering wheel.

"That was unbelievable. I can't believe we just made pasta. From scratch!" Andre says. He did *not* stop at one glass of wine, and his attention to his navigation duties has all but vanished. He's running a highly appreciative replay of everything we just did.

"Andre, does this look like the place we turn?"

"I don't know. Maybe? I think so?" He says, squinting at the sign. "Pretty sure." He looks around quickly and then relaxes back in his seat. "Yes. Definitely."

"That was quite a range," I say, laughing. "From 'I don't know' to 'definitely' and everything in between."

"That's life, Lazy Clay. That's just how it is. 'I don't know' to 'definitely' and everything in between."

"Such a philosopher."

"Well, that's why everyone back home calls me Socrates."

"Really? They do?"

"No," he says and laughs some more. "Melina, no. C'mon. You didn't really fall for that, right?"

"They should call you *'idioot,'*" I say and take my hand off the clutch to smack him playfully in the chest.

"Oh! That word I understood," he says and holds up a finger. "Idiot, right? They actually do call me that one."

———

INSIDE THE HOTEL, the lobby is a ghost town. Even the front desk sits empty. It should make us less worried about how loud we're being since there's no one around to disturb, but for some reason, it makes us whisper instead.

"What now?" I ask. I look over at him and he doesn't say a thing. Just locks eyes with me.

Oh, man. I hate it when he does that. Trouble always follows.

Over the years, my mother has told me stories about how I came to arrive in this world. She's a woman who looks at things with an unflinching eye, but even she gets a little soft around the edges when she recalls seeing my father for the first time, when she remembers those early, heady days in their relationship.

"Melina, your father was the most beautiful thing I'd ever seen in my life. It wasn't just that he was handsome. The Netherlands are full of handsome men. But your father, he had a quality back them—maybe still does, I don't know. It's probably what makes him such a good salesman. I was hooked before I even knew there was bait in the water."

I feel like that now. As if Andre is already reeling me toward him, with that impossible smile.

"Glass of wine?" he asks, holding up the crate containing the wine bottles I bought from the vineyard before we left.

"Sure. We probably should drink some of it. There's no way I can take it all back on the train with me," I say.

He's staring at my mouth when I talk, and the effect of that gaze is making me lightheaded and muddled. Drunk without drinking.

"On the train. Back home to the Netherlands. In three days."

I sound like a lunatic.

"You're not too tired?" he asks.

I look at my watch. "No. It's only *half elf.*"

"Beg pardon? What did you call me? Did you say 'half elf' just now?"

"Half past ten," I say, quickly.

"That's not what you said."

"Yes it is." I bite my lip to keep from cracking up.

"No, you said *'half elf.'*"

"Right. Half past ten."

"One of us is drunk here. It's probably me."

"It's definitely you," I say.

"*Half elf* is half past ten?"

"Yes! Why are you making this so hard?"

"That's what Half Elf said," he said and giggled at his own confusing joke. He explains it, but I still don't find it as funny as he does. "I crack myself up."

"I have some catching up to do. Let's go find some glasses."

"Right behind you."

"That's what Half Elf said," I venture, and Andre has to put down the crate because he's laughing so hard.

"You catch on fast," he says.

I'm so pleased to make him laugh this hard. This flirting, the sound of his infectious laughter, is more intoxicating than any wine. I'd forgotten how much fun this part can be. The moments when everything is new and undiscovered.

We erupt into the kitchen. Somehow, the quest to find a wine opener has become an unspoken race. He finds it first.

"Wait," he says as he holds it up. "Are we about to break another one of your rules?"

"Another one?"

"Yeah, first we weren't punctual, so the hostels were all full. The 'be on time' rule, broken. And then you told a lie to the front desk guy."

"I didn't lie to Emanuele!"

"You absolutely did, *honey*."

"Okay, I suppose I did. Now give me the opener, *sweetheart*."

I reach up to grab it from him, and we're nearly face to face, our bodies only centimeters apart. He holds it up over his head, but I'm almost as tall as he is, so I reach up and wrap my hand around it.

"What happened to the 'be direct and honest' rule?" he asks.

"Broken, I guess."

"What about not making a spectacle of yourself, drinking too much, et cetera?"

"Who's here to see me? No one." I say.

"I'm here."

"So close your eyes. Don't look."

"I want to look. I like looking at you."

I swallow hard. My lips fall open. I haven't kissed anyone besides Henk in so long, I've almost forgotten the panicked, aching anticipation that comes before lips meet.

The shallow breath. The flutters in the belly. The over-whelming need.

He lowers our hands, still wrapped around the wine opener, releases it to me and takes half a step back away from me and the wine on the counter.

"I'm trying to remember: did Pandora's Box have a cork in the top by any chance?" It sounds like a joke, but his voice is serious.

I'm already removing the foil and attempting to pierce the cork with the opener. "What nonsense are talking about now?" I ask, flustered, but trying to play it cool. My hands are shaking.

He closes the distance between us again. I can feel his eyes on me, but I keep staring at the bottle. I watch him wrap his long fingers around the bottom third of the bottle. I look up at him. He holds out his other hand gently, and I lay the opener in it. He slowly slides the bottle towards himself without taking his eyes off of me. I watch him turn his attention to the opening of the bottle, twisting the screw into the cork as it yields to the pressure he's applying. It goes right down the middle and is buried to the hilt before I know it. In one smooth motion, he pulls the cork.

The *pop* echoes throughout the kitchen like the first cannon shot fired in a revolution.

And so it begins.

CHAPTER NINETEEN

Each word is like a small bird pecking at my skull.

"Melina? You okay?"

Andre is not nearly so perky this morning. He's still be perkier than me, but that isn't saying much. His voice is flat and pained.

And it's not coming from the sitting room, but next to me in the bed.

"I need water. Do you want some?" he asks.

"That would be nice. Thank you." I uncover my eyes and accidentally catch the back of his t-shirt falling over his back as he puts it on. Were those scratch marks or just wrinkle marks from the sheets? I am not about to investigate.

"Did we drink all the wine in Italy?" I ask.

"No, but we put a serious dent in what you bought," he says, lifting a mostly empty bottle from the floor next to the bed and holding it up into the light.

"Als ik ooit weer iets drink, mag iemand me officieel opsluiten," I say, slapping my hand back over my eyes.

"That doesn't sound good. Let me guess: 'I'll *never* drink agaaaain.' Did I get it?"

"Close enough."

I hear him filling a pair of glasses from the vanity with water from the bottle included in the room. It sounds like heaven. It sounds like the answer to some of what ails me.

He brings it back to me, and I sit up to take it from him. "Cheers," he says and clinks his glass to mine.

"Wait, is it bad luck to toast with water?" he asks.

"Who's toasting?" I say, holding the full glass in my hand.

"Whoa. I thought regular morning Melina was grouchy. Hungover morning Melina is another beast altogether."

I look at him, make him meet my eyes.

"Be honest with me. Tell me. What do you remember?" I ask.

"The rules are back, I see." He sits down next to me on the bed.

"The rules are very much back."

"I remember everything." He brushes my hair back off my face and tucks it behind my ear. "And even though you are the grouchiest morning person I have ever met, you are still as beautiful as you were last night."

He drops his hand onto my knee. "How about you? What do you remember?"

I comb through my memory. A sexy slide show flickers in front of my mind's eye. The first hungry kisses. The tortuous wait to get to the room, which felt far enough away that we had to stop multiple times to tuck into corners. Hands everywhere. Mouths and tongues and breath. And that was just the trip back to our room. I flush and smile, remembering what awaited us there. Reliving those moments and all the ones that came after.

"Did you just…smile?" he asks.

I laugh and hit him in the chest. I cover my mouth and pretend to glower at him.

"Too late. I already saw it. What a great time to be alive. No one will ever believe it, but I saw it. A morning smile out of the High Priestess of the Morning Ogres." He raises his arms in the air like a victorious prizefighter.

He kisses me on the forehead and stands up. "I know better than to push my luck, though. I'm getting out of here while I can."

A mix of panic and embarrassment washes over me. I didn't know what I was expecting, but I didn't anticipate that things would come to a screeching halt like this.

"I'm going to go hop in the shower, and then I'll run down for another breakfast tray. I'm not brave enough to see you hungover *and* deprived of a bucket of espressos," he says, and walks toward the bathroom.

Relief floods my body.

"Can I ask why we felt we needed to drink that much wine?" I ask, laying back into the pillows and smiling (unobserved) to my heart's content.

"It was your idea, Lazy Clay," he says and cranks the water on in the shower, letting it warm up. "You just kept saying, 'no rules!' and pretend to tear up an imaginary piece of paper. And *then* you would hold out your wine glass again."

"But did you have to fill it every time?" I ask.

"You are a very, very hard woman to say no to."

The way he says it makes me feel swaddled in affection. Like a treasure worth keeping.

Then why did Henk have such an easy time letting you go?

I mentally shove that thought away with both hands, but not before it leaves a mark. I roll over onto my side, pulling the covers around me. I fall back asleep to the sound of shower water and Andre humming a Christmas song from the radio last night.

CHAPTER TWENTY

The breakfast revives me faster than I could've had any right to expect.

"So should we go find your luthier today?" I ask. "I just need to go around and do some sightseeing, but that can happen at any point over the next few days. There are a couple of places where we can have our meals comped if we want, but other than that, I'm wide open. We should have time to go find him, if you'd like."

Andre stands up from his chair and walks over to me, still sitting on the couch. He reaches his hands down to me. I put my hands in them and he pulls me to my feet. We're standing face to face and the look on his face is unmistakable. He pulls the collar of my sweater over and kisses the top of my shoulder.

"What happened to going and finding the luthier?" I ask with the little bit of breath I have left.

"Who?" he says, kissing my neck. "What's a luthier?"

It takes no further coaxing to convince me that the sights and delights of the Lang can wait until tomorrow.

Especially once the guitar comes out of the case. And I can kiss the guitarist anytime I want.

And even as I watch the hours tick by, knowing that by this time next week I'll be back home and this will all feel like a crazy dream I had once, I don't mind.

Because even if this is the only day I ever get to have this, it's still mine. It's ours. No one can ever take it away from us. And the notes that Andre plays and the love we make and the whispered secrets we share will be as etched into my soul as anything else that's happened to me so far in my life or will ever happen.

———

I WAKE up and see the sun already falling out of the sky. Andre sits propped up against the opposite side of the bed, guitar resting across his lap.

"Did you play me to sleep?"

"Yep."

"Did I snore?"

"No," he says. "But you do talk in your sleep."

I sit up. "Yeah?"

"Yeah," he says.

"Did I say anything interesting or wise?"

His guarded, sad smile says everything.

"That bad then?"

"Henk wouldn't think so."

"Oh," I say, blushing, feeling exposed. "Well, it stands to reason. Our break up was very…" I search for the right word and settle on "Recent."

"So recent that you're, maybe, still technically together?"

"No." I shake my head. "Henk and I are broken up.

He ended it with me." The words cut as I say them, scar my heart with the simple brutal truth of them.

"How long ago?" he asks.

"Why are you asking me this? And, honestly, what right do you even have?"

"What do you mean?" he asks, even more guarded now.

"What was it you said that time? About you and Amber? 'It's almost like you are apart more than that you're not together?' What about *you*, Andre? When exactly did you and Amber break up?"

He looks caught, sad, embarrassed, confused, and angry all at once.

"It's like I said. It's not that clear—"

"So with you and Amber, it may be as simple as a temporary geographical problem. Isn't that right? One that might be solved the moment you go back to America? Or one that wouldn't exist at all if she hadn't gotten into Harvard at the last minute and had just come with you as planned? Or if you had just waited to come with her another time?"

His face tells me I'm right. I go to the place we both know is inevitable.

"And then you and I likely never would have even met. We certainly wouldn't have ended up here together," I say, gesturing to the room, this bed. "We both know that's true."

He nods and chews his bottom lip. I let my words stand and wait for him to respond.

"I'm sorry," he says finally, quietly. His forehead, usually smooth, now creases. He looks like the picture of a conflicted man.

And so very, very young.

It hits me fully. This time with Andre has been like a scene in a snow globe that will never change. And from time to time in the future, I know I will dust off the memory of these days and give it a little shake, recall the beauty of these moments, this connection. But I will live outside the snow globe. And so will he. We're not right for each other. Not really. We were like two people stuck in a lovely purgatory waiting for our exes to meet us where we are.

"Nothing to be sorry about," I say. I lean forward to cup his face. Kiss him. Feel tears welling, surprising me with their intensity. I do hate leaving this lovely time behind.

"This is all my fault," he says.

"No. These have been a series of decisions we both made. I'm a grown woman, you might remember. I'm no victim here, and if my math is correct—and it is—the 'crazy ideas' have mostly been mine."

He shakes his head, laughing once. "There's some truth to that, but—."

"Listen to me. If these are bad decisions, then they are the best bad decisions I've ever made. I would do it *all* again. No regrets."

"Do you really mean that?"

I sit back and make an exaggerated offended face. "Are you questioning my ability to be honest and direct?"

He laughs, and it's looser this time. "Okay, okay." He takes my hand, kisses it. "I wouldn't ever want to hurt you. You are amazing, and you deserve so much."

"You haven't."

He turns his face mostly away from me, looks at me skeptically.

"You haven't," I say.

He looks like he wants to believe me more than he

actually does, but I've done everything I can. The rest is up to him.

"Can I ask you something?" he asks.

"Sure."

"I obviously don't know Henk, but I feel like I have a sense of just how devastated he *should* be to lose someone like you, let alone break up with you. How did that all go down, if you don't mind me asking?"

"It's, you know, complicated."

Andre looks at me with a patient, expectant look on his face. After I leave the silence between us unmolested, he breaks. "So you don't want to talk about it then?"

"He's a good bit older than I am."

"Okay… And?"

"And lately, there have been little things we've disagreed about. No one thing was a huge deal, it just… added up."

"Like what kind of things?"

"We've gotten into a very settled routine. And there's a part of me that worried that I was getting 'old before my time.' I've been feeling like maybe I should be out there… doing things."

"Like what?"

"I don't know. Maybe travel more? Traveling isn't really Henk's thing, so I've been pushing him to get outside of his comfort zone a little more."

"Seems reasonable."

"It is. But I think he thought I was wanting to explore my wild oats—"

"Sow your wild oats."

"Whatever the expression is. The more important thing is that I don't think I have wild oats."

"Oh, you have wild oats," he says. "Believe me. I have really, really enjoyed them."

"Don't try to charm me right now," I say, half chiding, half kidding. "I'm very vulnerable."

He holds up his hands in front of his chest, palms out. "I wouldn't dream of it."

"The thing is, most of the time I *like* knowing what I'm going to be doing every day and when I'm going to be doing it. I like that Henk is the most reliable, sweetest man in the world—no offense. You're wonderful."

"None taken."

"And I don't think I would mind going back to the life we had. Maybe it was a bit boring or quiet, especially for some people, but in many ways, it was perfect for us. It was perfect for me."

"Are you sure you wouldn't be shortchanging yourself, though? Settling? Maybe Henk was right?"

"I just don't think I'm cut out to be this wild girl. It's been fun, but I could never keep this up. I'm an old soul, with or without Henk."

"So what does that mean?"

"It means I will go back to my regular life, or at least what remains of it. Most of the time I will be in Utrecht with my job and my routines and my hobbies and just… spending time with my friends and my coworkers and my mother and my grouchy, over-bearing grandmother." I say and chuckle. "It means that while sometimes I'll go visit my father or go on work trips like this—well, not like this."

We smile at each other and stare for a long beat. There's no question that there is something here between us. It wasn't nothing. It's just not enough for either of us. I break eye contact, look down for a moment. Gather myself. Look back up. "But mostly, I'll be home. Where I belong."

"And Henk?" he asks me. "Will he be there?"

I take a shaky breath. "I don't know if we can find our way back to each other. But I have to try."

He just stares at me for a second, then nods. "I get it," he says. "I do. And it's not like I was expecting…" He trails off and waves his hands around. "It's just that it went by so fast, you know?"

"It really did."

"Yeah."

"What about you," I ask. "When do you go home?"

"I don't know if I ever will go back home, really. I'll visit, but I still have a lot to figure out. I just don't know what's next for me. I only plan as far as the next music festival at this point. That's about what I can handle right now. That's about all I've got."

CHAPTER TWENTY-ONE

MONDAY, 23 DECEMBER 2002

We spend our last day driving around without a destination and talking without an agenda. Sometimes I take pictures for the article. Sometimes a story from one of our lives makes us laugh so hard, we have to pull over. We find a restaurant in a small town that's open when we're hungry, and I eat the best sweet potato gnocchi of my life.

We get back after a final dinner out and once again, the lobby is empty. We go back to the room and down bottle after bottle of sparkling water. And cup after cup of coffee and espresso, even though both of us should be resting up for our travels. He teaches me how to play poker. I teach him how to play Pesten. "Oh, man, this is just like Uno," he says.

Cards and cups and mugs litter the coffee table between us. We sit cross-legged on the floor, and do our best to straighten out the confusing parts of our lives through a conversation riddled with jokes and a handful of teary moments and stubborn silences.

———

"I CAN'T BELIEVE I'm leaving you alone on Christmas Eve. Are you really going to be okay being alone for the holidays?" Andre asks.

"I really will."

"I could change my plans."

"You could, but you shouldn't."

"Why not?"

"Because the friends you're meeting in Umbria will be disappointed. And because I need to do my job. As a colleague, you're a mixed bag. A good partner-in-crime, but very distracting," I tease.

He gifts me a one-sided smile and then says, "I just hate to think of you alone on Christmas."

"It's not as big of a deal for me as it is for you. We do our biggest celebration in The Netherlands on December 5th. I already celebrated the holidays with my family and friends."

"For real?"

"Yes. 'For real.' We exchange gifts and have our big dinner on *Sinterklaasavond*. The other days are smaller affairs. That's why this is such a good topic for a Dutch travel magazine article. Christmas can be a great time for Dutch travelers to experience bigger Christmas Eve and Christmas Day celebrations in other places."

"Wow. I did not know that."

"Now you do. So you see? Nothing to worry about."

"I'll miss you," he says, looking at his hands just like he did that first time we sat across from the table drinking *Bicherins* in Torino.

"I know. Me, too."

"God, I'm so wired," he says. "That was way too much caffeine."

"Not for me," I say. "I'm fading." In reality, I'm well past exhausted. "Will you play me to sleep?"

"Anything you want. Name it."

"Busker's choice."

He chuckles once, sniffs, and picks up his guitar.

I drift off to a short, dreamless sleep on the soft notes of "It Came Upon a Midnight Clear."

CHAPTER TWENTY-TWO

CHRISTMAS EVE (TUESDAY)

In the morning, we take turns in the bathroom splashing water on our tired faces. I'll be staying on another few nights, but Andre needs to be dropped off at the Acqui Terme train station by ten. I pick up his guitar for him, while he shoulders his heavy backpack.

As we pass by the front desk, Emanuele stops us. "Hello, Ms. Jansen. I have a message for you."

"You do?"

"Yes, a man came by yesterday evening, but I left for the day before you returned. I'm sorry for the delay."

My stomach drops. I recognize the handwriting on the outside of the envelope. I'm too nervous to open it right now in front of Emanuele and Andre.

"What did this man say?" I ask.

"He asked where you were. I told him that you and your boyfriend had gone out sightseeing for the day."

Boyfriend.

"What did he look like?" I ask, even though I fear that I already know the answer.

"A little taller and a little older than Mr. Thompson, but otherwise, they looked very similar. At first, I thought perhaps it was your father, Mr. Thompson, but then he was only asking about you, Ms. Jansen."

The slim envelope in my fingers suddenly feels as heavy as a lead bar. "Thank you, Emanuele," I say. "For the note"

"Anytime," he says. "Are you ready to check out? I hope you had a memorable stay."

———

I WALK out the door of the hotel, the cold air assaults my skin, but helps for a moment to offset the hot panic I feel growing inside me. We load everything into the car, and each slam the doors behind us. The sounds of the seatbelts clicking into place are as loud as thunderclaps.

"Are you going to read it?" Andre asks.

"I'm afraid to," I say.

"It's from Henk, isn't it?"

"I can't believe it is, but I also can't imagine who else it would be."

"Were you expecting him?"

"No! Obviously not. He made it very clear we were finished. And that he was too busy at work to come on this trip with me."

"Shit, shit, shit."

"You know what?" I say. "I'm not going to read it now."

"What? Are you serious?" Andre asks.

"Yes. There's no time. We need to get you to the station to catch your train."

"Melina, it doesn't matter. If I'm late, I'll figure it out. I can take a later train. Maybe it would help if I was here to clear up any…misunderstandings…about us."

"That would be something to see," I say, raising an eyebrow. "No, whatever needs to be explained, I can explain just fine on my own. And anything that's in that note can wait until after I've dropped you off. It'll all be okay. No matter what, it'll be okay. I'll be okay."

I'm not sure which of us I'm trying to convince.

———

"I HAVE ONE PARTING REQUEST," I say, navigating the now familiar roads to Acqui Terme.

"I'm sorry," he says. "I'm not taking requests right now. I'm off on a busker's holiday to go see The Winter Jazz Festival in Umbria. Maybe you've heard of it?"

"I hear good things about that place. A friend of mine has been raving about it ever since I met him."

"Must be a cool guy."

"He's alright."

"Will you be performing there?"

"Not this time, sadly. I'm going to hear some elite music and maybe figure out what I'm going to do with the rest of my life."

"Seems like the perfect place to do exactly that. Now, about that request."

"So persistent!"

"Be quiet. Listen carefully. Here is my request. When you are rich and famous and playing before adoring crowds…"

He makes a sound somewhere between a scoff and a laugh. "Yeah?"

"Just once, maybe you could say, 'This one goes out to Lazy Clay—'"

"Okay, sure."

"—The Wisest Woman in All of the World."

"I mean, the wisest?"

"Maybe not the wisest," I say. "Given everything."

"How about the 'This one goes out to Lazy Clay, who only makes the best mistakes and brings out the best in everyone lucky enough to cross paths with her?'"

"That's pretty good," I say, a mix of affection and gratitude making me a little teary. "And if, you know, you want to say something like 'the stunningly beautiful Lazy Clay,' I won't be angry with you."

"What happened to the whole 'don't stand out' thing?"

"Everyone wants to be beautiful, Andre. And, besides, this is you making a fuss over this 'Lazy Clay' person, not me. I don't even know who that person is. I'm Melina Jansen."

"Yes, you are. Melina Freakin' Jansen, the coolest customer in all of Italy. Now when are you going to read that note?"

"The second you're on the train."

———

I HAND him his guitar case, and give him three kisses goodbye in the Dutch fashion. Just like I would to any of my friends. For once, we're both quiet. No smart comments or teasing nicknames.

"Thank you," he says. "And good luck. With Henk. With everything. I'd say look me up, but I have no idea where I'm going to be. Maybe sometime I can look you up? Visit you and your regimented life in the Netherlands? Follow almost all of the rules while I'm there?"

I nod. "Goodbye" won't find its way past the knot in my throat.

We step back and offer each other watery smiles. I tilt my head toward the entrance leading to the platforms, and he turns to go.

PART 4

ALBA, ITALY

CHAPTER TWENTY-THREE

I return to my parking spot just outside. I climb back into the empty car and tear open the note.

> Melina
> Sorry I missed you
> Henk

After reading it once, I toss it aside and throw the car into reverse without checking first. It earns me the first of many angry horn blows from local drivers. I give even the most daring and experienced Italian drivers a few scares on the drive back to the *agriturismo*. I hug the curves of the winding roads and accelerate to pass at every opportunity before finally skidding to a stop in the parking lot.

Hurrying up to the desk, I ask Emanuele, "Were there any more messages for me? Did anyone call?"

"Yes, signorina. That same man called."

"What did he say?"

"He said he would see you in Alba."

I go back out to my car and dig out the address to my next hotel. And then, inspiration strikes. I drop into one of the chairs in the lobby and text Ingrid, hoping to mine her for information and/or advice.

> Henk is in Italy!

> What? REALLY? Miracles never cease.

> Did you know he was coming?

Dots appear like she is typing. Then disappear. Then reappear. And disappear again. Finally, her message comes through.

> Long story

I dial Ingrid's number.

"What do you mean 'long story'? I'm not waiting for you to peck all that out on your phone."

"Melina, are you calling on your cellphone? Are you roaming? This is going to cost a fortune."

"Well, then you'd better talk fast. What are you not telling me?"

"I may have run into him last week and given him an earful about being a coward and letting you slip through his fingers."

"Did you tell him about Andre?"

"The hot American guitar player? No, of course not. I didn't even know about him then. I'm not even sure you'd met him at that point," Ingrid says.

"What is he doing here?"

"Your guess is as good as mine, but I'd say probably being brave and trying to win you back. What did he say when you saw him?"

"I *haven't* seen him. He stopped by the *agriturismo* while I was out, and the front desk clerk told him I was out with my 'boyfriend.' He left a note for me, but the clerk just gave it to me this morning."

"What did it say?"

I read her the note.

"That's it?"

"Yes."

"That's it."

"Where's the other guy—"

"Andre."

"Where's he? Is he still there with you?"

"No. I drove him to go catch his train this morning."

"So it sounds like you have *a lot* to tell me sometime when you're not racking up roaming charges. I don't have any useful information for you, so let's wrap this up for now. Call me when you get to your hotel in Alba."

She hangs up before I can protest. There's nothing to do now but head to Alba and see what awaits me there.

CHAPTER TWENTY-FOUR

The drive to Alba only takes about half an hour. It's a pretty trip that I know I'm unlikely to travel again soon. I won't be visiting this corner of the countryside again, so I try to savor it.

But the pull to Alba is strong. And even though it's scary and confusing, and I am a ball of nerves and missing Andre all at once, there's something steadying about the idea of going to Alba. For the simple fact that Henk is there. And for the last few years, until very recently, he was my port in the storm, not the storm itself.

Arriving in town, I find comfort in the flat, narrow streets. No expansive views, but no harrowing drop offs either. It's a place more like Utrecht in that way. It makes me realize that despite the indescribable beauty of the Langhe countryside, I'm still a little homesick. I'll take my comforts where I can get them at this point.

Pulling up to my hotel, I find parking for my car. I don't bother to take my stuff inside, but just go in to the front desk to check in. I confirm with every single one of the clerks there that I don't have any messages waiting for me. And citing and following hotel protocols—something Emanuele at the *agriturismo* clearly isn't as familiar with— they refuse to confirm whether or not Henk is staying here.

I haul my stuff in from the car. Once again, my room is a welcoming and comfortable space. Not as sumptuous as the Torino room. Not as expansive as the *agriturismo* room, but comfortable and draped in history and charm. And empty.

I make myself put things away, thinking establishing any sort of order in all this chaos might help me think straight. I try not to take the silent hotel phone personally. I turn on the radio, but the Christmas music reminds me too much of Andre and his guitar, so I snap it off.

I do what everyone does when they're out of ideas. I call my mother.

"Hallo, Mama."

"Melina! Where are you?"

"Alba."

"How is it?"

"I haven't explored it yet, but I'm sure it's going to be wonderful."

"Have you been having fun? How were your adventures in the countryside?"

Mam has a way of saying things she doesn't know have a double meaning. I burst into tears.

"Mel, what's wrong?"

"I'm just…it's been an amazing trip, Mam, but very confusing and hard trip, too."

"How else could it be at this moment?"

"What do you mean?"

"It's the holidays, which are always full of highs and lows under the best of circumstances. And you just broke up with Henk—"

"Henk broke up with *me*, Mama."

"That's what I meant. Break ups are hard, but…"

The silence on the line is pregnant. I can tell there's something she's not saying. Mam would never let this much time go by when she knows I'm paying for long distance. "Mam, what are you not telling me?"

"Is it…have you had any surprises?"

"You knew Henk was coming here?" I say. "*Why* wouldn't you tell me he was coming?"

"Why would I spoil the surprise?"

"To warn me?"

"Why would you need to be warned?" she asks. And then after a beat, "Ohhh."

"Yes, Mam."

"Well, how could I know that?"

She has a fair point. There's nothing for me to say to that.

"Was it terrible?" she asks.

"It was…nothing yet. I haven't seen him."

"I'm so confused. If you haven't seen him, then how do you know that he's there?"

"Because he left me a note."

"What did it say?"

"It says, 'Melina, I'm sorry I missed you. Henk.' That's it. He left it after the desk clerk told him I was out sightseeing with my boyfriend."

"*Oh mijn god*. You have a lot to tell me when we are not paying by the minute. Is 'your boyfriend' still with you?"

"No. He's gone. To Umbria. He's not my boyfriend. He's just a friend." Already Andre is starting to feel like somebody that I used to know more than someone I will probably ever see or know again. A year from now, he will be like a half-remembered dream.

"Wait," Mam says. "Read me the note again."

I don't need to pull it out to read it. The words are burned in my brain, so I say them again.

"Does it say, 'I'm sorry I missed you.' or 'I'm sorry. I missed you.'?" Mam asks. "Because those are very different messages."

"I don't know. Let me check." I realize that it's not here. I would tear through the room to find it, but I've already put everything away. I *know* it's not here. The last time I remember seeing it, I'd thrown it to the side in my car. Hopefully, it's still on the floorboard or something, but I can't be sure even of that.

"I don't have it. I left it in the car. I just thought he was angry and leaving me a passive-aggressive note calling me out for being with someone else," I say.

"You should find that note. But even if you can't, let me ask you: when have you ever known Henk to be passive aggressive? He's never been anything but direct and honest with you. Well, maybe except when he broke up with you—"

"Mam, what do you mean? Are you saying he wasn't being honest with me about something?"

"No. I'm not saying another word. You can ask Henk about that when you see him. I've said too much already."

"So you're saying he was saying he was sorry and that he missed me?"

"You need to find him, Mel. This is a conversation you need to be having with him, not me."

"But how can I do that? I don't know where he is. He doesn't have a cellphone. I don't even know how he found me. Ingrid said she didn't tell him, and we were already broken up before I even booked the trip." It finally dawns on me. "*You* told him where I was."

"He asked me. And when he did, of course I did. It's Henk, not some stranger."

I sit on the edge of the bed. My head feels clearer than it's been in a while, but it's still a lot to take in.

"Melina, we need to go. This bill is going to be ridiculous. If he calls me, I'll tell him you're in the Alba hotel. Beyond that, I don't know what to tell you. Good luck, *droppie*."

CHAPTER TWENTY-FIVE

Out of ideas and patience, I go back outside as the evening slides into the night. I bring my camera to keep me company, reminding myself I'm still here for an assignment. I wander the narrow, meandering streets snapping pictures here and there, but mostly looking for Henk's face. I suspect he's probably halfway back to the Netherlands by now, though. I know I'm unlikely to spot him out for an evening walk among the hordes out enjoying the festivities. I hope for it anyway.

I walk and walk, peeking into restaurant windows, just on the small chance that I might find him eating a late dinner alone. I try to spot him in the back of taxicabs that drive by with their lights off.

I stop into every hotel I pass, scanning the lobby. I approach the hotel clerks each time and ask if I can leave a note for a guest who *may or may not* be staying there. Even that earns me uncomfortable looks from the staff, highlighting exactly how unprofessional Emanuele's actions were. I leave notes with my cellphone number and my room number at the hotel, just in case, but I have little hope of any of them being delivered or paying off. And really, Henk should have both numbers already, anyway.

A crowd of runners passes me, carrying candle torch-lights and singing hymns. I step to the sidewalk to watch them go by, snapping some pretty good shots for an event I wasn't expecting to see. Their delight is contagious. I follow them, drafting on their joyous exuberance. It's exactly the kind of thing I'm here to do.

They run through the Piazza Risorgimento, which is in the heart of Alba's historic center. I've basically been making concentric circles toward this very place. The runners stop to sing a few final hymns in celebration before disbanding.

A busker takes the opportunity of an enlarged audi-ence to ramp up his playing. He belts out a cheerful saxo-phone version of "All I Want for Christmas is You" by Mariah Carey. Even though I'm surrounded by the sound of the music and the smell of the food from the few stalls still open and the white lights gracing the huge Christmas tree and the larger light show bathing the whole scene in an array of blue and gold, I feel like I'm behind glass, not really here experiencing it at all. It might as well be on television.

My swirling mind and my yearning heart crowd every-thing else out.

I snap photos, thinking some of these are so good that perhaps this will allow me to skip some of the other things on my travel itinerary. I could use a day under the covers, just unspooling from everything and regrouping. Along with perhaps a touch of wallowing.

When the crowd thins out, I give up and decide that it's time to go back toward my hotel. I know that sleep will elude me. And that I will probably get up in the morning and try again. For now, I'm exhausted. Tomorrow is another day, one way or another.

I feel out of place in this happy place, with the people around me so full of anticipation for what the Christmas holidays will bring. I drop a few euros into the busker's case on my way by, wondering if he, like Andre, is on his way somewhere else. He makes eye contact with me and winks, but I turn away without acknowledging it. Like we say back home, *"Een ezel stoot zich niet twee keer aan dezelfde steen."* A donkey doesn't bump into the same stone twice.

Though I don't think that my time with Andre was a mistake, I also don't see myself making a habit of such things—no matter what happens next with Henk. I like slow burns. The sparks and light that shoot off people like Andre burn too bright for people like me.

I hustle in the direction of the hotel, watching the way the light show dances along the walls surrounding the piazza and remembering how the Torino light show had charmed me. It feels like a long time ago now, though it's only been a week. I turn the corner, once more distracted by the sights and sounds of Christmas celebrations, and smash into someone.

This person I don't send reeling. He's far too rock solid.

And this time I don't go bouncing off either. Instead, strong arms steady me while I regain my balance.

Henk.

CHAPTER TWENTY-SIX

The reason I haven't been able to find him is because he wasn't here.

A man who loves to plan, whose job it is to organize other people and think entire seasons ahead about what might be needed, embarked on this trip with a small duffle and no reservations.

A man who loves the comforts of his home and his familiar routines got on an airplane and then a train and then a cab to come find me with nary a word of Italian under his belt beyond an awkward, "Ciao."

He doesn't have a hotel, because his only plan was to come find me and hope that I would take him back. Everything was closing, so we're sitting at a table in a far corner of the now empty lobby of my hotel.

And for once, the man who hates risk, whose primary art form is the creation of contingency plans, was left without a clear picture of what to do next.

"I don't even have a return flight until you're due to go back," he says. "The only thing I knew to do was to go to the places your mother told me you would be."

"That was your whole plan?" I ask.

"Yes," he says.

"So, then," I say, frowning. "Where have you been between Monday and now?"

"When the clerk and your hotel told me you were with someone else, I didn't know what to do or say. I scribbled the only thing I could think of and then left. Luckily, I had enough sense to ask the cabdriver to wait while I checked to see if you were even there. I just climbed back in and had him take me to the nearest hotel."

"You were in the Langhe countryside, too?"

"I could actually see your *agriturismo* from the place I stayed. I almost walked over so many times, but I needed time to think. I didn't want to make any more mistakes."

I'm so shocked by everything he's telling me, I have to lean back in my chair and give myself a moment to absorb it.

"When did you arrive in Alba? And why didn't you go to my hotel?"

"I did. I caught a bus from the nearest town, which took me longer to get here, but the cab rides were…" He winces, which says enough. "When I finally got here, I asked at the front desk of your hotel, but they weren't nearly as helpful as the man in the *agriturismo*. So I have just been walking around trying to work up the courage to go back and at least get a room in the same hotel as you this time."

"Who *are* you? I don't even know you. You look like Henk Havertong, but he would never do any of the things you are describing."

He shrugs. "You're worth a better Henk Havertong than the person I had let myself become. I don't want to be the kind of person who would let you go. That man is a coward and a fool." I notice the fine lines around his eyes, which still shine with so much warmth and decency.

"Why *did* you break up with me?" I ask. I twist my hat in my hands, but Henk gets even more still, which is his version of squirming.

"You always seemed too good to be true, Mel. Our relationship seemed too much to hope for, especially at my age."

"Henk, you're forty-eight and one of the healthiest people I know. You're not exactly at death's door."

"But look at you. You could be with anyone. You could be with someone your own age. Someone with more energy to keep up with you, who likes to travel and try new things."

"Henk, one thing I learned on this trip. *I* don't have enough energy to keep up with me. I really wouldn't worry about that."

"But you do seem like you were open to trying new things," he says.

His comment hits like an arrow in the center of a bulls-eye. And yet, I realize that it doesn't sting, because it is obvious to me that he's terrified, not angry or accusatory. For the first time *ever*, I understand that Henk is just as scared and fragile and foolish as I am, as most people are. He's just had more years to get good at hiding it.

Does he think that he can be so easily replaced?

"I was open to new things, because the one thing—the one person—I want was taken away from me." I lay a single finger on the back of his hand, which rests on the table between us.

"If that's still true. If that's still me," he says and curls his finger over mine, "Know that I'm here for you now. And I will never do anything to push you away again."

"No matter what may have happened with Andre on this trip?" I ask.

He doesn't wince at Andre's name, but he doesn't freeze either. Instead, he meets my eyes. "No matter what. He was lucky to be with you for a few days. I'm hoping to be with you for the rest of my life."

CHAPTER TWENTY-SEVEN

CHRISTMAS DAY

We don't say anything to each other. It's too early, and we've been up all night talking.

And because civilized people don't address each other until an appropriate amount of time and caffeine have been applied to the day.

It's Christmas Day, and the Alba church bells are pealing in celebration. Henk and I will find coffee and some incredibly delicious food. I will take some pictures and some notes for the article.

And then we will come back here to this bed and pick up right where we left off.

———

THANK you for reading Alba Home for Christmas! Don't miss the next romantic escape to the Langhe, *Truffle in Paradise!* A story of truffles, culture clashes, unexpected chemistry... and one very special dog.

If you're anything like me, you'll want to grab your

preorder of *Truffle in Paradise* now, while you're thinking about it, and then get that fun surprise later! ;)

If you'd like to keep up to speed on all my shenanigans, you can find more on my Substack newsletter list, "Friends in Leau Places" at https://79franklinpress.substack.com/s/leau-macy-readlaxing-romcoms.

PART 5

EPILOGUE

Bloomington Herald-Times
December 5, 2003

"Local Jazz Musician Shines on International Stage"
Byline: Herald-Times Staff

Bloomington native Andre Thompson, a proud graduate of Bloomington High School North and Indiana University School of Music, is making waves in the international jazz scene. Thompson, who graduated with honors from IU's prestigious music program, had the opportunity last December to sit in on an impromptu jazz session during the renowned Umbria Jazz Winter Festival in Orvieto, Italy.

Thompson described that experience as "surreal," sharing that the festival has long been a dream destination for him. "To be surrounded by some of the greatest jazz musicians in the world and to have the chance to play alongside them was incredible," Thompson said. "I knew it was where I belonged."

The opportunities flowed from there. Because of connections he made there, Thompson went on to study the intricacies of instrument craftsmanship with accomplished luthiers (master guitar makers) in both Florence and Milan.

In addition, Thompson secured a paid internship with the much larger festival that has taken place in Umbria every summer since 1973. Known simply as "Umbria Jazz," the festival requires a large number of people to coordinate the large lineup of musicians and manage the logistics of the event itself. "It's exciting to be involved behind the scenes, learning how a festival of this caliber comes together," he added.

Thompson credits his time at IU for preparing him for the challenges of the international music industry. "The Bloomington community and its love for music really set me on this path," he said. "I feel lucky to have grown up in a town that values the arts so much."

In between his work with the festival and honing his craftsmanship skills, Thompson has managed to release an EP called *Lazy Clay* available on MySpace, PureVolume, and CD Baby.

For more local stories about Bloomington's artists and achievers, visit HeraldTimesOnline.com.

THE END

FRIENDS IN LEAU PLACES

***Visit** 79franklinpress.com/leaumacy **to see what other books I have available or in the hopper!**

****Keep the conversation going by joining me on my Friends in Leau Places Substack!*** Get access to sales, promos, and giveaways from Readlaxing Books, tons of romantic comedy and chicklit book recommendations and reviews, and the opportunity to join "The Leau Down," my Advanced Reader Copy Team. Members of my ARC team receive FREE access to early releases, digital swag, and behind-the-scenes peeks on my work-in-progress.

****Want to Keep It a Bit More Casual, But Still Stay in the Loop?*** Find out about upcoming releases from Readlaxing Books by following Leau Macy on Amazon, BookBub, and/or Goodreads!

ACKNOWLEDGMENTS

Writing stories isn't as much of a solo act as a lot of people think. It might be one person at the computer, but we writers are surrounded by the lovely, patient people who put up with our shenanigans. The brainstorming. The half-distracted stretches, where we don't fully exit our imaginary worlds before trying to reenter theirs. The endless revisions. The full-on wrestling matches with imposter syndrome. I could go on and on. (And often do.)

So, as always, I remain grateful and lovestruck by The Fam, who stand shoulder to shoulder with me through all the peaks and valleys of this unpredictable, taxing, chaotic, and fulfilling profession. Being the mom/wife in residence at The Big Ugly is still the best gig I'm ever going to have. So, Fam, maybe you've heard me say it a time or two, but here it comes again: love you guys. So, so much.

I can't say it better than I've said it before: so many thanks to my friends and family who remind me to get out and live it up from time to time. Without them, my boss would have me working basically all the time. It is only through their steadfast commitment to coming up with a wide array of fun and tempting activities that I am saved from becoming a work hermit shackled to my desk by my love of this cray cray pursuit. You guys rock.

Robin Knabel, my O.G. partner in crime, constantly dazzles me with the vivacity she brings to absolutely everything she does. I'm not entirely convinced that she actually sleeps, but somehow she manages to craft the sort of fictional nightmares that all of us fans love her for. (All while doing ninety million things for everyone in her life.) Readers, if you want to walk on the wild (eerie, macabre) side, get yourself over to https://www.robinknabel.com/ STAT! RK, thanks for going on the joy ride that was Unsettling Reads with me.

Annie Marcus, my RAMP Mentee Sister from Another Mister, keeps me sane and laughing by bringing the exact ratio of level-headedness and humor to every situation. Nobody does it better. A.M, you are a bright, bright spot in my days. Not to be a nag, but as one of your biggest fans, I'm going to need you to get me that next book at your earliest convenience. For anyone reading this, join me in the happy, hilarious world Annie has created. Here's a map on how to get there: https://www. anniemarcusbooks.com/.

I dedicated this book to Karla for good reason. She's the writer, podcaster, mentor, and just all around badass known as K.L. Brady. Trust me when I say you need more K.L. Brady in your life. For me, it's been a game-changer. I'd start with her romcom novels and her podcast, "Chicks on Christmas Flicks," but she's got some spy thrillers that'll keep those pages turning, too. You can find more information on everything here: http://klbradyauthor.com/ (or wherever you get your books and podcasts). Like I said, she writes across several genres. If you got this far, I can pretty much guarantee you're going to find something you like.

And Karla, just know that when I do finally get to meet you in person, I'm going to be checking your back for wings when I give you one of the biggest hugs of your life!

And last, but not least, my readers. Thanks for taking a chance on me. I hope I gave you a brief respite, a pep in your step amidst all you're grappling with in your day-to-day life. That's pretty much my number one goal these days. Because these wise words from Ray Bradbury really resonate:

"So while our art cannot, as we wish it could, save us from wars, privation, envy, greed, old age, or death, it can revitalize us amidst it all."

Good luck with all *your* shenanigans until I see you next time!
Leau Macy

LEAU MACY

Leau Macy writes escapist, (mostly) closed-door romcoms in the WanderLove Series, where complicated wanderers find their happily-ever-afters in dreamy destinations. Her stories are designed to make you laugh, fall in love, and maybe check flight prices. She writes with the encouragement of her husband, sons, and two spoiled mutts. A sucker for shiny new projects, you'll find her picture next to "planning fallacy" in the dictionary. She fuels her efforts with iced green tea and questionably sourced optimism that *this* time the book won't take twice as long as she planned.

"Leau" rhymes with "go"

www.leaumacy.com